the long dry

Cynan Jones was born near Aberaeron, Wales in 1975.

the long dry

Cynan Jones

Parthian
The Old Surgery
Napier Street
Cardigan
SA43 1ED

www.parthianbooks.co.uk

First published in 2006

This edition 2007

ISBN 978-1-902638-93-5

Editor: Gwen Davies

Cover design by James Fleming
Typesetting by Lucy Llewellyn
Printed and bound by Dinefwr Press, Llandybïe, Wales

The publisher acknowledges the financial support of the Welsh Books Council.

British Library Cataloguing in Publication Data

A cataloguing record for this book is available from the British Library.

For Charm and Mum,

and in memory of D.LL.W.

Chapter One

the Cow

He tastes to her of coffee. In the morning, when he comes to wake her up.

'The cow's gone,' he says. 'The roan with the heavy bag. She's gone. I'm going to look for her.'

He walks out and though it's early there's a promise of heat in the sun. It's been like this for weeks.

She thinks of him walking down the lane, along the hedgerow, into the long field, the flies buzzing and ticking as he walks quickly over the dried ground, scuffing the loose stones.

He climbs over the first gate and she hears it clang gently through the open window of the room. She imagines him stopping; watching and listening, and all he hears are the flies and the flat moans of the sheep when they look up at him.

She looks at the watch on the table by the bed and it's just gone six.

—

the Calf

He'd woken earlier and gone out to check the cows. The night had been still and again he could not sleep with all the thoughts filling the silence of the un-moving night; so he had got up and gone into the clear, still morning. For very long it had been very still. It was before the light came up.

With the light of the torch he found the stillborn calf dead in the straw of the barn. He rubbed the stump of his missing finger. He could see the cows' breath in the morning air – which even then was cold – and a warm steam off some of their bodies. The mother of the stillborn calf was kneeling beside the calf lowing sadly and gently. The other animals hissed and puffed and chewed straw.

He took the dead calf by its ankles and lifted it from the straw that was bloodied by birth, not by the calf's death. It was strange because the mother had licked the calf clean. He thought of the mother cow licking her calf and not understanding why it would not stand clumsily to its feet, its legs out of proportion, its eyes wide. Why the incredible tottering new life of it did not come.

He carried the calf out of the barn, counting the cows inside, and went out into the field. Kate would be sad about the calf. The calves died very rarely for them.

—

Over the hills behind the farm the light started. Just a thinning of the very black night that made the stars twinkle more, vibrate like a bird's throat and put out a light loud compared with their tinyness. He'd noticed the missing cow.

He'd hoped it had got out of the barn and into the field, where there were other cows with older calves out. She was very close to calf and heavy and perhaps went because of the terrible thing of the still birth.

In the dark he could not see the cow and he carried the dead calf across the field, hard grazed because there had been no rain. Somewhere, a large truck growled along the road, near the land he had his eye on. He dropped the calf into the old well at the bottom of the field because he did not want Kate to see it and because it was expensive to send in the dead calves to find out why they died. You always lose some, he knew. There is no reason. You will just lose some. He hoped the cow had not gone missing.

the Farm

The farm sits on a low slope a few miles inland from the sea. Gareth's father bought the farm after the war because he didn't want to work for the bank he worked for anymore. The farm had belonged to an eccentric old lady who was found feeding chickens in her pyjamas by the postman one morning. She had no chickens. Three sons and her husband had gone to war and they were all killed in the war one after the other, in order of age. When they found her feeding chickens that were not there she was taken away and put into a home where she died of a huge stroke like she couldn't be away from the farm. When Gareth's father bought it, the farm was collapsing.

The family moved in with the intention of rebuilding, of refurbishing the farm; but after the first few frantic months they did little and settled into the place. Things took on names – the rooms and the fields.

In the new house, after the floors were re-done and the walls sealed and plastered, painted brightly, things were placed here or there – the ornaments and bowls. It was too deliberate, like posing for a photograph, and odd to Gareth who was young then.

When the house started to live around its new people, things seemed to find a more comfortable place for themselves – like earth settling – haphazard and somehow right, like the mixture of things in a hedge. They relaxed and walked round the house in their shoes. Before that, for a while, it had seemed to the children like the house was bewildered by the attention – it was like they were when their mother wiped their face with a cloth.

—

'I wanted him last night,' she thinks. 'Really. And then I don't know. It went away again. I went flat, like I was numb, when he started touching me, and I tried to be patient and coaxing but he could tell, so he stopped and he didn't say anything. I could tell he was angry. Not really with me, just, he's been very good recently not starting anything and then I started something. And then he knew I didn't want it; and I don't know why. I miss his hands. God, I miss his hands.'

She's started this, now. This way of thinking – as if she's talking aloud with herself, as if she is a face framed in a mirror talking back to her. A means of control, or of measure. Of trying to make sense. Women get old quickly, when they get old.

She feels her body moving under the rough cloth of his shirt, which she has thrown on to be out of bed. In the mirror, behind her, the unmade bed. She feels her body is soft and filled with water and dropping with age, and there is no way he can look at her now and feel the things he has felt for her in the past. He will want her because of his care for her now, not out of desire. It's like being allowed to win a game. He can't possibly *want* her body. She wonders about cutting her hair short again.

—

Sometimes they go funny. When they're fat with calf. They go funny and they do something, and it's impossible to guess what they have done by trying to think like them. Because they don't think when they do this. If they decide to go they can go a great distance. Just stumbling and crashing along and it doesn't make any sense. All you can do is try and find them and hope they are okay and do what you can. Stay near them. Check them. Mostly they're okay once the calf has come.

—

She was a dairy shorthorn – the only roan, which is a mix of red and white hairs that makes her look mostly red, the colour of bricks – the other shorthorns were white, or red, or white and red, but they didn't have many. Most of the cows were Friesians – the black and white cows of children's programmes that Emmy thinks look like jigsaws. They only keep a few cows now, after the quotas. They had milked many, but when the quotas came in they stopped after a few years because it was expensive to purchase the quota. Also, they had good cows with good butterfat in their milk and it was hard keeping the yields down, and you had to pay heavily if you overproduced. Many of the small farmers around them stopped dairying too, and left it to the big farms, which the quotas favoured. Mainly, they farmed sheep. They sold off a lot of the cows and kept a few for beef and, at first, for their own milk, but later mostly for stock cows. Gareth was glad they had kept some shorthorns because they were less greedy than the Friesians and were happier with feed. Without the grass it was hard to keep the Friesians fed.

—

Curly

He looks down at the dry earth and he knows that it has been too dry for marks now for weeks – for hoofs, or pads or tracks. His best chance will be fresh cowpat, or a crushed section of hedge where she has forced her big weight through. You would think it would be difficult for them to move with such big bags and being all heavy, but they are stubborn big animals, and they can go through things when they choose to.

He kicks up a small rough stone and uses it to saw some twine he can't undo without his finger. His Leatherman, he can't find. Emmy bought him the Leatherman on her own (her own choice), on the birthday after he lost the finger – saying it does lots so it can help be what your finger was. He loved his daughter for this – her way of making tragedies smaller, by finding answers, charmingly.

It takes something to break the twine and he thinks, gradually now, my strength will leave me. When he moves the gate it collapses and bends with a hard groan. He does not get angry with the gate and he looks out, over the sea.

That morning he had watched the dawn. The dawn coming up from the ground. A single bird was singing, like a child talking to itself as it plays. He had thought of the night that was ending, and of the quiet dead calf and the missing cow, of his father's memoirs which he is reading to help him sleep or stop him thinking of the other things, like the land he wants to buy, and of his wife's body; and he thought it was terrible how much he wanted her good body last night. Want will not diminish. It's an odd thing to keep secret – how much we want each other's bodies.

The harder mountains to the north stood out then, like knuckles at arm's length in front of your eyes and the mist ran down from them, rolling onto the long sea until it turned to cloud and lifted into the sky. The sea was like wet glass in the sun.

For a brief moment, at this dawn, there was coldness – like a final rush of breath, then warmth came. It came slow and full and sure, like it had done for weeks.

Now, still early, he feels the warmth on his shoulders and starts down the sloping field. The cow is not here.

Swallows tuck and dive in the corner of the field where a natural spring has made the grass thick and full, taking the dew from the lush blades.

He cuts across the field and cuts under the ancient blackthorn, twisted and aubergine, clinging to the dry soil of the bank. The stream is dry. Here and there the water rises from the deep ground making patches of mud dotted with bright green weed and the footprints of birds, but the water does not run. There is a scattering of broken shells around a sharp stone where a thrush brings snails to feed on. He likes to hear this, the sharp clear tick of the shells being broken on the stone. It fascinates him, the tiny ingenuity of birds.

He follows the line of the stream down and ducks under the fence which hangs uselessly between the banks. In the next field, where the pond is, swallows drink from the water and take the small flies that buzz in crowds while it isn't yet too hot. He remembers that he has forgotten that today he has to go and collect the duck. Perhaps he feels the breeze begin, a little. This year the swallows came early.

For a while the beauty of the pond and of the swallows holds him. Then, knowing the cow is not here either, he turns and starts back for the house.

—

In the winter months the water runs down the lane, bringing with it the dirt and stones. And these and the fallen leaves fall into the ditches and the drains so that after a while they are blocked and the water runs in sheets across the fields, feeding the fine grass and sinking into the earth, which is rich and dark here.

Down the lanes and in the hedges there are always gorse flowers somewhere, but they come thickly in the Spring. First the yellow – the celandine and daffodils, dandelions and primroses, then white – star-gazed the anemones, clouds of snowdrops, may blossom and stitchwort – colour coming in schemes at first to the wide land, before other picks of colour – the dog violets, and the bluebells and campions, and, in the woods close to the stream, wild garlic. On a day like this – with the faintly lifting breeze shifting off the sea to the south-west, across the fields –

the smell of garlic sharp and sour and wonderful would come across the farm, earlier in the summer. But the flowering is over now.

The dog, Gwalch, has followed him down the lane, and he stands lean and young by the gate. He is a sleek and ready and strong dog. Further up the lane, he'll find Curly, the big old dog curled and resting in the sun on the path, half-way down, which is as far as he could go now. The dog had started happily and with hope and had gone down the track after the younger dog and then just got tired and lay down in the sun.

The old dog looks up as he hears the curl of a car engine shift quickly down the road across the valley. Gareth hears it too. There is a nice hunger in him, and he wants coffee now. The house is blinding on the hill.

He looks down at his feet and sees the lime gathered on his old leather shoes. The lime has not gone into the field because there has been no rain. He looks at the field and the hard earth and pads it under his foot. He's worried about the grass; it's not good to be feeding hay at this time of year, with the young lambs and the calves coming. The animals need fresh grass. He knows too, that when the first rain comes it will wash away the lime and run off the dry broken ground.

She drops the bacon into the hot pan and it snaps in the boiling grease and starts to curl. She puts the bacon she has already cooked on an old plate and puts it into the warm oven to keep warm. The bacon in the pan is spitting and cracking noisily and she turns the heat down. The kitchen starts to fill with a weak blue smoke.

They built the extension themselves, turning the old kitchen into a place to eat. Even now the walls are damp in the morning as the house sweats out the heat that comes into it in the day. The wallpaper lifts in chunks from the wall like bark coming off and there's velvet-looking mildew here and there, all somehow unimportant and right and of no worry. They don't notice now. The old house has these, like a tree does.

In the kitchen there is a stove with gas bottles illegally close to it. There's a small window, thick with condensation, which is permanently open but still mists, and a calendar of farm scenes from a stockfeed manufacturer. There's an old Belfast sink against the wall, and from this a pipe runs outside through the wall to an outside tap with half a foot of stiff green hose attached. Underneath the tap the moss and green mould grows thick and well.

The Formica units are always clean, so you can see the strange wary pattern on it, and above them, above the plastic pots of sugar and tea bags and constantly pilfered biscuits, chipboard cupboards hang somehow, heavy with half-used things and tins of beans and fruit that are never used.

She sweeps the tiled floor while she listens to the bacon snap.

The kitchen extension falls from the room where the food was originally made. They call this room the kitchen too, from habit, but everything happens here. Here is the settle and the family table, and the big window which looks back at the rough, secret half of the farm. Here the post is opened and the meals are eaten and, when it is done, the homework is done. All the talking.

The tiles on the floor are different from the tiles in the new part, which are red and made of brick. Here the tiles are old flags of stone which she loves secretly because of the colours they become under the careful wet care of her mop. Sometimes she likes to think that only she sees this, because they only show their colours when they're very wet, and they quickly dry while she moves across the floor. This childish energy is still in her, somewhere; a glee she hides.

Here and there are piles of dirt. Little crowds of dust and dropped things, like the foil from pill packets and pennies and hairbands bright with dust. It's a process she has while she waits for things or she talks worriedly. She takes the brush and moves the dirt around the floor, leaving it gathered here and there. Later, she will take the dustpan and clear them up; or the cat will come and attack them and fight them furiously. Depending on her mood, she will either laugh or shout at the cat.

She leaves the brush by the doorway and takes the bacon out of the pan and puts it in the oven on the plate. The doorway goes out of the kitchen onto the back yard of the house and it's where the family and good friends mainly come in and out, during the day. Below the units are sacks of potatoes and tubs and bowls of cleaning things stacked up. The front of the fridge is rusted and pocked but the fridge works. Old and out of place, a chest of drawers fits beside the fridge and holds knives and forks and things.

As she cuts the bread thickly to put in the pan she wishes for a new kitchen. A kitchen gleaming and clean; but mainly she wants cohesion. She is tired of mixed up things.

Behind the house, across the small back yard of broken concrete, the land slopes up. For a while there is bracken, dead and dry now from the long summer, and then the slope sharpens and the forest starts. The leaves are very heavy this year. To the side of the house, where the ground is even, more or less, there is a lawn of sorts and a small rockery made with stones from some of the out-buildings they never rebuilt. The lawn goes along the big edge of the barn and loses itself where the bramble starts before the forest. She opens the door to let the house breathe and looks out at the lawn.

—

the Vegetable Patch

Where the bracken is now, on the slope, they worked hard when they were younger to take this for themselves. First they cleared a break, so the fire could not spread into the trees, then they burned the bracken and bramble and the thin shoots of hazel that had come out of the forest. They did this at the end of summer. Then when the ash and the broken wood had been driven into the earth by the thick rains of Autumn, they began to dig the ground. They dug for a day, and hurt themselves. The next day he hired a rotovator and they cut up the half-acre patch of ground which was still tough work. The smell of the rotovator reminded him of boat engines. The robins were the first to come and take the grubs and worms, and worked around them. Then, when they were inside taking a cup of tea and talking gently together, the bigger more cowardly birds came. The earth was full and hungry.

The frosts fell and nothing grew in the earth. Then, when the winter loosened, they dug the broken soil over to give it air and make it ready for the seeds.

They planted seed potatoes, and cabbages and long rows of onions and beetroot and radishes. They had carrots and parsnips, which needed to be thinned constantly and were a lot of trouble, and pea canes and lettuces. Even with the failures, they had a lot of vegetables. Too many for themselves. They also put in raspberries, still there now, but you had to fight your way to them. Then at some point, and she tries to think quite when, they didn't plant things anymore and the woods took back the land. It was after the second miscarriage, but she does not remember that.

—

the Finger

Inside she sets the table. The knives and forks and plates in piles on the vinyl cloth. She starts to read her catalogue of supplements; things she hopes will stop her ageing, help her hold less water, help her be less tired and make her want sex more. For her age, she is a very beautiful woman, but she does not see it. It is beginning to go from her. She knows it.

He comes in, scraping his feet on the metal grill outside the back door, not because he needs to, but from habit. Or perhaps it is his announcement – a signal they have always had but never spoken of. They had many of these when they were younger.

She rinses the cafetière and warms the cup with water from the kettle which she's boiled several times while she has waited for him. She does not make the coffee. Some things she mustn't do. She's threatened by the coffee; about how strong to make it, how it tastes when it is made. He makes coffee every day, just for himself as no one else drinks it. He makes a strong pot full of coffee at this time of the morning and it does him for the day, warming up the cupfuls in a pan as they are needed – which makes them stronger as the day goes on. No one else touches the pan. She says it's why he does not sleep. His first coffee each morning is the remnants of the night before because grinding the beans he does not want to wake the house, and the children sleep above the thin ceiling of the kitchen.

He sits at the table with a loose fist and runs his thumb over the first joint of his forefinger in the way he has, so it makes a quiet purring sound, like rubbing leather.

'What about the dosing?'

'It'll have to wait,' he says.

He rubs his finger. He does this always, at table, talking, or reading a paper, even with the handle of a cup held there, so that this part of his finger is smooth and shines. Whenever he's at rest.

'I don't know,' he says. 'I've checked the obvious places and she's not there. She's got her head down and gone.' He does not tell her about the stillborn calf.

'It's typical. It has to be today,' she says. 'I should have got up to check.'

'It would have gone anyway,' he says quietly.

He looks down at the missing part of his little finger on his right hand and makes the sound against his thumb again. She still blames herself for this damage to him. He was trying to free the bailer from the new tractor and she had done something and the catch had just bit down. He takes a mouthful of coffee. It was a clean cut and it healed well and he could have lost his hand instead. That's how he looked at it. In some ways he loves it.

She'd burned the toast so he's gone quietly over and made some more while she tried to rescue the wrecked toast.

'The vet phoned about Curly,' she says.

'Oh.'

'He wants to come today.'

He knows the vet will put the old dog down. Not today, he thinks. It's a hard thing to have to have today, if he has to find the cow too.

'You should have some breakfast,' he says to her. It's odd how seriously we take the silly names of animals.

The door latch snaps and Emmy comes in still dressed in her pyjamas and her blanket tucked in her hand, thumb in her mouth. She shuffles over to the old settle and curls up with her green and purple zebra. She would come down when she heard her parents talking in the kitchen below in the morning.

'Hello sweetie,' says her mother.

She shines her eyes up at her mother, looks to her father quickly, shyly. Something secret passes between them and she smiles and settles. They stop talking of the cow.

He sits there rubbing his finger and looking at the stump of his little finger fondly.

'It's going to be hot again today,' he says.

*

Chapter Two

the Rain

There had been much rain. In the early part of the year and through the Autumn before, the rain came down and the fields were loud with grass and the rivers full and fast.

Then at some point in the early morning of March 11th something changed. The rain stopped; that day the sun came out hot and fast and deliberately. There had been a geomagnetic storm. Epileptics had fits, and people prone to strokes or with weak hearts were ill, some died. The electric things of our body went wrong in many people. The swallows came early, and that day a cloud of racing pigeons and one white dove landed at the farm. They came suddenly and curiously and were very lost. Emmy fell in love with the long white dove.

Nobody – not the 'experts' anyway, admitted any link between the storms and the sudden change of things; but storms like this could shut down warships and satellites, and the War Office was always watching out for them. In their records, it says the storm on March 11th was a massive one.

Then it rained in May. He remembers the shearers – three men – moving methodically around the barn; the process: the unspoken movement of them all.

—

The rain came down on the tin roof and the shears buzzed slightly. It was very calm.

The three men – a father and two brothers – came only to shear the sheep. They made a living this time of year moving round the farms, taking the fleece off the sheep and taking the money per fleece. So they worked quickly. The fleeces came off and Emmy and Dylan and Kate gathered them and rolled them into bags, fastening the canvas with wooden pegs. Gareth caught the ewes, and Bill helped, while the shearers worked quickly. (His name was Gwilym, but they called him Bill.)

Now and then the men would stop to oil the shears, or, the sheep still held sitting comically against their legs, would reach languidly behind them for iodine so they could dress any cuts, if they had made them badly. They were quick but moved easily, as if their bodies were made only for this purpose. They might have been – a long line of sheep shearers. Genetic. When they stopped to eat there was no talk. Pleasant thank yous, humble and clear, but no talk. They were men with no unnecessary thing.

*

Chapter Three

the Ducks

He'd got in at three in the morning and he wasn't happy about going to get the duck.

'You'll have to go and get the ducks,' his mother had called up. 'The cow's gone and you'll have to go and get the ducks.'

Dylan shouted and then swore at his mother because he knew his father was out in the fields – he'd heard him go out after breakfast again to find the cow. He'd sworn quietly at first so his mother had to shout up 'what did you say?' and then he'd repeated it at a scream because he knew it annoyed her more this way.

He was angry but it was mainly out of habit; and he was only angry because of getting out of bed not because of having to go and get the ducks.

Now he was in the Transit and he drove it quicker than he'd drive his own car down the busted lane and enjoyed the tuck and muffled rumping of the ducks in the bread crates in the back. With the windows down the smell was still bad but it was good to be in the Transit.

If you've never been in a Transit you don't know. You sit up high like you're in a dining chair and there's even arm rests if you want them. And you see things you haven't seen before or don't see often. You can even see more of the road somehow, and because you're up high you're not so scared. You're not scared when you drive a car maybe, but you know if you hit something it will more or less hit you at eye level and it will be like being shot out of a low pipe at the mess.

He was relaxed and happy in the Transit.

He drove the van past the barn and down the track and into the long field. The ground was so dry you could take the van in the fields. When he got out to open the gate into the long field he did it angrily in case he was seen. He thought he should be angry because he usually would be because he had to unload all of the duck on his own; but he wasn't angry and driving the van was good and the heat of the day was already in him and quietly he loved being in this place despite the belt of the music and the white breasts of the club last night still hefting round his mind. He had to like the club and he had to want to go away from here.

He took the duck down to the pond.

—

Every year they put a hundred duck down on the pond. There are already moorhen on the pond, and coot. Other wild duck join them, and teal – small and dart-like things that are beautiful and fast and violent, not at all like ducks. They feed the ducks grain and cut down the reeds so the fox doesn't get to them without them seeing, and they care for them deeply. Then they shoot as many of them as they can.

This is a good thing. Ducks can be a menace.

People are seduced by ducks; by their seeming placidity. They fall for the apparent imbecility of their smiles and their quietly lunatic quacking. But they are dangerous things which plot, like functioning addicts.

In the local town – a beautiful Georgian harbour town which is not lazy and which is very colourful – the ducks got out of hand.

The river comes in from the low valley, collapsing slowly over the old weirs, under the road bridge and into the harbour to the beach. There's a place on one side of the road bridge where you can sometimes see the current going backwards when the tide comes in, and there are sometimes big crabs and mullet in the salt part of the water. And the ducks come down the river.

As part of a move to make a continent look better, money

was given to the small town to improve itself and they built a holding pool for the smaller boats and fishing boats that would still work in the winter when it was too rough to have expensive things like yachts still in the harbour. The holding pool filled with ducks and they shat everywhere. There were hundreds of ducks. Sometimes you had to stop your car to let them cross the road.

Given the way they have to have sex, it's remarkable there are *any* ducks. More remarkable they have sex often. The male more or less drowns the female, who has to focus hard on staying afloat, and they both have to deal with wings and beaks and water and feathers and it looks nasty and they still have sex. So there were a great many ducks. And they all shat everywhere.

It became a problem for the tourists and the locals didn't like it. People talked about the ducks in pubs; and if you stood in lines at the local shops you heard people talk about ducks. About the latest violence they had committed.

If you tried to drink a quiet pint on the harbour the ducks were there and they sat squatly and looked up at you and seemed to chuckle superciliously, which was off-putting. If you put your washing out, somehow the ducks knew, and by some defiance of physics managed to crap on it. And duck crap isn't nice. It's green like baby-shit. If you fed a baby on broccoli for a week.

The ducks were all over the expensive yachts and got in around the car wheels and even climbed into prams or anything that was comfortable and abandoned. Cats were scared of them and they wouldn't run away from children so children didn't chase them. They even sat stoically through the frankly vicious din made by the local band who played hymns on the harbour every Sunday night. They seemed to be invincible. A committee was drawn up.

The reason why they shat so much thought some of the committee, was because 'the people' fed them chips, whoever 'the people' were. A duck should eat things from the water, that's what they're designed to do. But they were lazy and so hoovered up whatever people threw them, fighting off the seagulls and the errant starlings and the pigeons and, if they had to, fighting off each other too. This poor diet is making the poor ducks poo. That was one take. Answer: we should give them proper food. Genius. So they tried. It was not the answer. They ate the food put down *and* the fish and chips and had sex even more. Ducks' arses were no tighter than they'd ever been. There were simply too much ducks.

Shoot them was another angle. Poison would kill every other thing, and the ducks would go on living, cunning as they were. So shooting was the only sure-fire way.

Now it's legal, more or less, to shoot a duck yourself, provided it's below the line of the low water. Or so the fable goes. It's one of the many rules few people really know. At this point the duck belongs to the Queen – a spurious ownership anyway. Unless she's there, the chances are she wouldn't know or wouldn't mind. However, no one's ever done this and you wouldn't want to be the first. If you walked around a quiet Georgian town blasting ducks you'd be quickly locked away.

And this was the chief qualm against the 'shoot them' plan. Shotguns are very noisy and would not be good for business. If you opted more subtly for a hunting rifle there'd be another problem: you'd simply be too close. A rifle is designed to counter a human's lack of tact: it kills things far away. If you shot a duck from far too close with one of those machines you would obliterate it. Which would make as much mess as the poo, only harder to clean up.

So eventually they laced the food with rampant contraceptive. Looking around the town nowadays, it's a shame they didn't lace the chips.

Another case against the ducks – or some might say for – is simpler. The farm where he had picked the ducks up in the Transit is on a low hill overlooking the bay, constantly plagued by fighter jets. The Americans and lots of other people come to practise flying here and when they do, it sounds like they are tearing up the sky. Sometimes they are so low you feel them; and you can always tell when there is some trouble because they practise harder, and in the night you can hear the heavy hum of Hercules planes shifting things around.

When a jet goes over low at calving time sometimes a cow will drop its calf and it will be dead and unready. If you call for compensation, they ask you for the number of the plane and the exact time it passed over the cow. On average, the jets travel three times faster than sound.

A duck went through the windshield of one of them, macerating itself into the cockpit and the pilot ejected. The navigator flew the plane and landed it safely two-hundred miles or so north. Bits of the cockpit were spread for miles around the hills and didn't hit anyone and a team of Crash Investigators came. Again, ducks.

He backs the Transit up by the pond and it makes a sound just like the one he used to make when he was being a truck when he was a child. The crates are heavy full of duck and the stink is bad. It stinks like the insides of a fish and it's been cooking slowly in the back of the van. He puts the crates down one by one by the edge of the pond then cuts the twine with a Leatherman he found in the van and makes the ducks go out. They're not sure what the pond is.

They pat into the water one by one, confused and fik fiking. In the crates they were bunched in, bunched into themselves and had the stupid air of herd animals. When they get into the water they are confused and then they kick a little and feel themselves glide and feel all their clumsy weight turn easy. Then their necks lift and stretch and some of them flick their clipped wings and they turn into proper ducks; a real thing. It's their first time in the water.

He watches them. Damselflies and strong white butterflies, delicate as hell, are everywhere around the pond, and machine-like dragonflies hit smaller insects in the air as they fly. The reeds are flowering with their strange crests and on the island in the middle of the pond the willowherb is starting to come to seed, and the thistles.

From now on in the evenings he'll come down here, sometimes with his father, and whatever has happened in the day will be okay. They'll try uselessly to count the ducks and he'll watch the light change and sink into the water – the white light of a lake. The evenings will shorten and the flowers turn to rough seed and the grass will stop growing, not that it's grown much this dry year. Then, if there is rain, the mushrooms will come which his sister loves to eat because she believes in fairies, and they will take bags down to collect them and most will not get eaten and will sweat and go off in the plastic bags.

He lifts the bread crates back into the Transit; he's old enough to sweat now and it's very hot. Everyone is still bewildered by the heat.

He gets into the Transit and turns it on and likes the growl of the diesel engine. He presses down on the brick of the pedal, swings the van away from the pond and smacks the radio on loud to smash away the quiet place – the beat breaks out, bass line, moving up his spine. And his head fills up again with tight breasts and bare arms and small skirts and white skin bluing in the epileptic lights. He's not little now, he knows, and he has to want to go away from here.

Gareth felt the cool wind the speed of the quad bike made as he rode to the top fields. He knew now that if he didn't find the cow soon it would become a problem. I should ask Bill to help find the cow because he will like helping, thought Gareth.

He had seen the bank yesterday, and they had agreed in principle to his putting in a bid for the seven acres of land that skirted the road, close to the top of his farm, close by this field. The auction was next week. Gareth thought about it a lot.

It was the other side of the road from his land and ran in a long strip about an acre deep. It was where the road was quite wide, and close to the village. He wanted it to build on. At least, he wanted to sell the land as plots. He knew it wouldn't happen soon, and hoped the idea wasn't thought of, or he'd be easily outbid. But if he could get the land, and then get planning, he could make a lot of money. The village would grow, and he knew physically that he could not farm forever.

Far away, he heard the duck go into the water. 'If I can get that land,' he thought, 'when the village moves this way I'll file for planning.' (They'd already put in speed limits, as they do before allowing houses to be built, though they don't admit it). 'I can get planning and sell the plots, and it will be a few years from now and then I can rent out the top fields and some other land and keep the farm like an island, without having to work it all, because I won't be able to; and the plots will bring us money, if I can get that land.' He hoped very much that the agreement from the bank would be enough.

He thinks of his father's memories that he reads at night to help himself sleep. To bring some sound into the stillness. How it is difficult and slow to understand sometimes; how the dictionary does not have the words he doesn't know; how he must make bridges of meaning, here and there. As if he were walking on stones down a river. He prefers to call them memories, because memoirs sounds too grand, too fake.

Mopping his brow with the rolled-up sleeve of his shirt he thinks of the building land and how his father used to work for the bank he's borrowed from, though the bank has globalized now. How, from reading his father's memories, he is beginning to understand the reasons why he gave it all up – this good career – to bring his family here, to bring them up on the land. It's unnaturally quiet up here, in this sun. Things are exhausted.

A story he read some nights ago comes back to him, strange against the heat now, crystalline in its difference. Its difference to everything else in his mind; clear images standing out, like a photograph in a white room.

—

the Angel

He knew the place, even today, from visits to his father's family years ago, where the water goes under what used to be a beautiful low stone bridge before it was rebuilt for no apparent reason. On the high side of the bridge, upstream, there is a constantly still pool, hollowed into the deep shale. The waterfall is usually quiet, unless there has been a great deal of rain washing from the fields, into the river, swelling the water. It falls only eight foot or so, into the pool. The other side of the bridge the water bubbles away over shallow, broken rock.

His father had been with the other children at Ysgol Sul, the Sunday School, in a small room by the chapel. It had a blackboard and a brand new gas heater which gave off a thin hiss the very sound of which, ever since, would be enough to clothe his father with the illusion of warmth. It was a very hard January - the seasons then were more severe, or else his father's memory had sharpened them. They wore shorts then, too, of course. His father was one of the oldest children there.

Tommi Falch came in late, a boy of six who said he'd seen an angel in the waterfall: '*welais angel yn yr rhaeadr.*' He said it like a boy coming on in a school play. Whenever Tommi spoke, his father remembers, it seemed he had rehearsed, which gave him a gladness, as Gareth imagined, reading the memories, to be like those tragic children in films who delivered sentimental lines with crushing but accidental poignancy. He said 'I've seen an angel in the waterfall.'

Tommi was to see an angel again, years later, when he lay dying in a bomb crater towards evening during one of the last days of the war, not feeling any pain from the wound that had torn off his arm. A man ran past with a shard of metal, blast-whitened in his back, ripped and shaped like wings. 'Angel,' said Tommi, as his life levelled out.

He was a tiny and scared child and he still looked mesmerised and stood talking quickly, opening and closing his hands while he told the preacher, Tegla Davies, what he'd seen. The preacher listened quietly. His father wrote how it always seemed he was listening to a far off sound. There were eleven of them at the school that day and not one of them would ever forget the thing they were about to see.

Outside there was a vicious frost and the preacher took them out to see the angel.

The preacher was a man whose mellow voice and stern fervour gave him effortless control over the children and they were quiet as they walked. There was no malice meant for Tommi in taking them to see a thing which could not possibly be there - he didn't for a moment want the boy to look a fool. Clearly, Gareth's father reflects, the preacher would have been thinking of some lesson, some didactic: how God could manifest Himself in many ways; how angels could visit, pehaps, a pure enough mind, even in the beauty of water. He was successful at getting the children to believe in God, not by forcing them to believe, but by showing them things which would make it almost impossible not to. For the first time in their lives, they felt the quiet excitement of grown ups.

When the preacher reached the bridge he stopped and held on to the bluestone wall. He was trembling. The ch ildren filed around him. The tiny riot of the stream below them and the falling sound of melting where the sun fell thinly over the hoar frost, and the preacher shaking. These are the things his father remembers most. The waterfall was frozen. And there in the ice, where the fall began, was a girl, catching the light like spider thread, with her white shawl spread out around her in the frozen water.

It was years before they were told she had drowned herself because she'd found she was with child and in his father's village they talk about it to this day. This story stood out for Gareth. He'd seen a lot of things die, and none of them beautifully.

—

He left the bike at the top of the lane and walked into the long field that crested the hill. They called this field Top Field. Over the road was the plot. He could hear Bill's tractor ticking close by.

—

Bill

Bill had lived on the next farm and grew up with Gareth. He had a very pretty sister. Bill was simple.

When Bill's father died they had to leave the farm because they found out they did not own it. It hadn't belonged to them for years. Bill did not understand.

Bill's father had invested heavily in pigs. He borrowed from the bank to build pigsties and a place where he could kill and salt the pigs, which is a hell of a business. Pig farming was a very different thing from cattle and sheep, which he sold, but it seemed the clever money back then.

They had long kept just one pig; would feed and fatten up the pig then slaughter it and slowly the children came to accept this process (only the head scared them, whenever they found it, and when they sneaked into the cool pantry and opened the brine barrel, the grey distended cuts of flesh floating in the water would always disturb them). Their father decided to develop a pedigree herd of Welsh pigs – a strong, long pig with long wide ears and a long jowl and he protected them mercilessly from the invading Landrace pigs, which came in from Sweden around the 1950s and which, to the general wisdom, were a good thing to start breeding into your stock. He farmed the pigs outdoors, and his fields were scattered with the corrugated iron farrowing arcs which Gareth's father said reminded him of Nissan huts and airfields. (This picture amused Gareth – squadrons of flying pigs).

Even when the Welsh breed opened up its herd book for a time in the middle of the 50s and encouraged the introduction of pure Landrace blood, Bill's father held out – despite the accumulating problems of maintaining sufficient male and female lines while avoiding inbreeding. It became more and more difficult for him. To keep the blood lines fresh, stock had to be imported from several sources, which was always a risk, and gradually, without a doubt, the number of pure pigs was decreasing. He borrowed more and more. Meanwhile, over-production of low-quality pigs – the very thing he fought against – almost collapsed the market and herds declined in line with their fall in profitability.

The herds which had cross-bred cleverly still stood; the improved carcass quality and production efficiency of the scientifically-bred Landrace enhanced the originally hardy constitution of the old Welsh breed and made them economically viable, reducing Bill's father, who had never hybridised, to the standing of a hobbyist. Eventually, his fight for purity backfired. Increasingly, piglets were born with defects, all with cartoon names – 'splay leg', 'kinky tail', 'blind anus' – all harking back to some sexual deviance. In desperation, in '57 he introduced a line of Landrace boars, hired in from across the border. Ironically, they were of Danish origin, rather than the Swedish stock:

the Danish strain had already caused great problems out in Canada. The pigs born developed raised lesions on their skin, had broken hooves, died easily of pneumonia, and it took some time for the local vet – a cow man, really – to diagnose the hereditary *Dermatosis vegetans.* Everyone was pretty sure the semi-lethal recessive gene responsible lingered in the Danish pigs.

He fought through it more or less but then a few years later pigs started to simply die. They diagnosed swine erysipelas – the thing they call 'the diamonds'. The germs that cause this can live in piggeries and on 'pig-sick' land for years so it was assumed the pigs that came in brought this. In one form of this disease, the skin discolours into raised purplish areas, which at first looked like the dermatosis again, so they did not treat it properly. The purplish areas run along the back and over the flank and belly and look like diamonds, more or less, which is where the sickness gets its name. In the chronic form, the pig's joints are affected, causing lameness, or the germ attacks the heart valves, making cauliflower like growths on them until they fail and the pig dies. The vet looked at the dead hearts and gave his misdiagnosis.

The pigs were becoming recognisably 'depressed', went weak, then collapsed and died within a day or else died suddenly. It was really Mulberry Heart disease, and the second, younger vet confirmed this when he found the bloated, mottled livers and hearts lacerated with haemorrhages.

The herd was culled and any of the good meat sold. Bill's father gave all the money he could to the bank and a few years later shot himself.

Before that happened, another farm bought the place and broke it up. They used much of the land themselves, but let the family stay in the house for a rent, and farm cows on some of the land. The family never knew the place was not theirs anymore, their father kept that from them.

When the old man died and they couldn't work the farm anymore, the big farm sold it. They had to move into a small house in the village but Bill could not adapt. Gareth would find him walking round the old place, mystified, at night; or in the day, amongst the unused outbuildings as they were then, and around the boarded-up house.

So Gareth's father gave some land to Bill. He fenced off a few acres by the road and said to Bill it was his land now, and he could farm it. So he takes the orphaned lambs and grows things there and helps out on the farm when help is needed, like at shearing time – and he cuts grass for old ladies in the village and takes people spuds and cabbage; but underneath, as Gareth knows, he doesn't understand still.

—

Gareth didn't expect to find the cow up here. But he needed to check, to rule this out, because it was easier to search here. If she was not here, then he would have to check the bog. He did not want to think that the cow was in the bog and he hoped he would find her here but knew that he would not. He wanted to find her before the vet came for Curly. Being in the top fields he could hear the cars coming and would know if the vet came down the lane because he knew the sound of the old vet's van. Then he would have the bike to get back. He knew she was going to have a calf but somehow he didn't care about the cow inside and was more worried about the way Kate would be and the things that would happen if he didn't find her. He knew that he was looking in the top fields in case the vet came and he knew inside that the cow would not be here, and that he should look for her in the bog.

*

Chapter Four

He lies awake now – so still at night – and I know he's thinking of the unhung gates, and the dead grass, and perhaps of how fat my body is. Other nights, reading, reading, reading. By the bed light he looks at his father's diary – not a diary. A collection of things he remembers.

I think it is hard for him to read the diary – the memories that were handwritten by the old man. He has to decipher the writing, and the Welsh sometimes, because it is a difficult language often, even for the people who speak it. He has Dylan's old school dictionary by the bedside, and I can hear him scrabbling for meanings as I lie beside him, when he thinks I am asleep.

—

the Farmhand

After the first miscarriage she was not well. It was strange because Dylan had taken strongly, and had grown full and vibrant and well inside her and she had not suffered any loss before him as many women do – as if their body cleans itself by flushing out the unused mess of ten years or so, so it can begin fresh and rich and make the healthy baby of a clean young body. It was then the headaches started. They were rare, but they were very bad.

They continued to try, first easily then with more need, to give their son a brother or a sister. She miscarried twice. On the third time they told her she couldn't have children then. She was thirty-four and damp like Autumn, not wet in the way young women are, like Spring, but damp and rich and earthy, and it didn't seem right that she could not have a child. She was fertile and hungry, like fallen leaves.

When she took the farm hand she was angry and possessive. Gareth was away from the farm that day.

The farmhand was younger than her and blue-eyed and heavy and Gareth had taken him on because after the miscarriages her headaches had grown more frequent and Gareth wondered if it was because she could not do the work. She loved her husband very much but she was in the shed and the farmhand was there.

When he touched her she kissed him hard and pushed against his hands and when she tore off her jumper so he could see her full breasts he looked hunted and scared of what he had started. She took him in her hands and got out of her clothes and let him take her against the filthy tyre of the tractor.

When it was done she felt sick and he was sitting on a bale in shock, and she grabbed her clothes and her Wellingtons and ran barefoot and crying over the yard to the house and in the bathroom she was sick over and over and she cut herself for the first time. Gareth found her sitting in the shower with the long cut on her arm starting to clot. She wouldn't speak to him.

It was two years before she was well again but she still feels sick now when she thinks of what she did, and the nagging doubt haunts her sometimes. It has never been the same since then. He blamed it on the miscarriages.

—

Emmy

It was hard to bring up Emmy with Kate being ill. He had taken her from the shower and cleaned her cut and they had made love very gently after crying together. Kate cut off her hair, so it was all short and severe, and still talked very little; and when the pregnancy held past the more dangerous months Gareth was very happy. Emmy was born in the Spring.

—

Water

Gareth cuts across the open fields, knowing the cow will not be there, and crosses the hedges where the gaps are wide and dry. He can see in the dry bank the places that have been dug by badgers, and their beaten path. In the blackthorn, or here and there around a fence, you can find the stiff grey hairs, touched black and white, if you look.

You can see as well the trail of hay and straw they steal from the feeding troughs to make their bedding which they keep meticulously clean, or the pads of red bracken. There's a tree he knows, an elder, where they go to clean their claws and keep them sharp, taking off the damaged parts and the caked earth on the rough bark of the tree. This is close to the set, and he's very secret about where the badgers are, even though they can bring disease to his cattle and his land.

In the third field down, close to Bill's plot, a wide strip of bright green grass follows the line of an underground stream which goes down to the river. There are a lot of good springs on his land, he is lucky, though this year even they are too little. Even so, he has to pay a tax each year for the water he takes from his own land. They flooded valleys full of farms and villages once, to give water to towns.

—

Rachel

He sees Bill climb onto the old Fordson tractor and they lift a hand to each other. If you look at him now, he looks emaciated; has dissolved almost to the point where he looks as if he's held together by his clothes. On his plot, amongst chaotic sheds full of his tools, sometimes you feel he could simply dissipate into the clear air, like so many dead leaves. It's strange for Gareth to think that he's seen this man more or less most days of his life. He hasn't seen his sister for years.

She was small and pretty and when her father shot himself she was sixteen. She did not like her mother, who could not tolerate her growing up, and she left home to become an air stewardess. It was as if she wanted to refute things utterly. The hold of the land on the people who grew up here. The hold of a meaningful place.

Gareth never forgave himself. She was one or two years younger than him and he'd rescued her more times than he could ever remember. From pirates, Red Indians, dragons. She grew up expecting to be taken away.

One day they were in the hay barn hiding. He can never remember what from. They weren't old enough yet to realise that, actually, they had started hiding from nothing, just to be together and feel their hearts quicken, with their breath held and them both trying not to pee.

They were at the top of the hay and there were mouse droppings and dry, pasty white bird droppings and feathers and white shafts of strong light coming in on them where the barn slates were broken. Their skin itched and stung in the hay pleasantly. She was lying next to him in a blue check dress that she wore all through the summer – and if it got dirtied it had to be washed so she could wear it the very next day. Not knowing why, he felt his penis come awake and though he went red and tried to hide it she saw it stiffen in his shorts. She made a quick exclamation as she saw it move and closed her top lip widely; then she put out a finger and pressed it. He was incredibly embarrassed. It had happened very suddenly and it was bewildering. He climbed down from the hay and ran off. Nothing ever happened between them again.

—

the Mole

Four days ago Kate found a mole. The cats had brought it dead into the kitchen. They never eat them, because the taste is bad to cats, but they bring them in as gifts. It always amazed her how clean moles were, with the velvet fur which can brush either way. She was angry at the cats for killing something beautiful and blind but they didn't understand. If they caught a rat they got a plate of milk.

Kate threw the mole behind the barn and the flies found it. The green flies which feed on the wounds of sheep and lay their eggs in them this time of year, so the sheep have to be dosed all the time. They laid eggs on the mole as it began to stink. The skin on its face and hands dried up and stretched and beetles took it so half of the face was bone now and you could see the teeth. The eyes go first. Sexton beetle larvae broke down the meat and guts and the things inside and soon there was a hole in the side of the mole and the flies buzzed round it constantly. Even small birds came and took maggots that were feeding on the mole to feed their chicks, and took fur as well, to line their nests.

The beetles too ate the fly maggots and dug a shaft below the mole and dragged it some way down, rolling off the skin so some of the mole was in the ground and was above too. It was too big for the beetles to use totally. They laid eggs close by and fed the hatched larvae with partially digested bits of mole. Later, the beetles bit an entry hole in the rotting carcass and helped the growing larvae in. They fed themselves.

When much of the goodness of the mole was gone and the bigger insects went the ants came, cleaning the bones and the lining from the skin, and taking the weak maggots. They worked beautifully, with blind obedience, blind as a mole until all the mole was gone with them into the ground again, and only some parts of bone would be left if you found it now.

—

the Cats

She sees the cat cut slyly across the lawn. The cat had long been tormented by the gentle terrorisms of the children. In defence, he had adopted a placid, somewhat bourgeois cynicism; he also smouldered with the simple fury of having had his balls cut off and in defiance of his emasculation paced about the place with the slow steps of a tiger: it's a threatening ability in nature to look like you can put down great weight gently.

The other cat, whom Emmy had insisted on naming ridiculously, used different tactics, she being a she. She was beautiful – a tortoiseshell with teardrop eyes and the inbuilt mischief anything with lovely eyes has naturally. She loved Gareth, and seduced him every chance she got. She was frivolous as only the beautiful can be. She was the hunter.

The other cat brought bigger things in, like baby rabbits and once, remarkably, a seagull, as if to say 'if I wanted to I could'. But the constant offering of small rodents and slow birds were brought by her.

There had been a third cat, a sister, but she was gone. She was weaker from the start and, as she would, Kate loved her the most. She went missing at hay-making and no one wanted to believe that she had gone under the machine, so they decided to accept that she must have been kidnapped by holidayers, as happens. Gareth was convinced the dogs next door had taken her.

Fire

Gareth comes back along the road in case the cow has broken through the hedge, but he knows she has not. There is no sign of her. In the hedge, bordering the piece of land he wants to buy – he sees the houses in his mind – is the dead black ash of old fire. All summer there have been little fires in the hedges where people have thrown cigarette ends from their cars. They throw out the cigarette and drive on, as the flame curls and starts and rips up the very dry grass of the bank into the brittle hedge. It takes nothing, this year.

He wonders if the vet will come. Curly now is very old. He's had him since he was a pup.

When Emmy was very small she used to drag the dog round by his ear, as if she were using him to help her walk. They joke that the dog taught her to walk, not them. Now he is very old and can't clean himself properly and has developed a painful lump the size of half a football on his side. Yesterday he was bitten by a rat, so the vet has to come now. It is time.

—

He goes over the style that joins the footpath cutting through their land – the strange, ambiguous green arrow – and as he lands he turns his ankle. It hurts sharply for a moment, and he suddenly feels tired and angry. He can't stop thinking of the dog. Often, the ground here is crossed with tracks – foxes and cats, walking boots and strayed sheep. Now there is nothing – no sign of movement; just the deep shape here and there of a horse's hoof made long ago, when the mud was wet. The immoveable fact that the cow is missing begins to anger him as he follows the footpath, the shock of his ankle slowing to a dull pain. He must be very careful with his anger because it is very big when it comes.

The footpath runs between two hedges for a while before breaking out into open land, following a line of blackthorn down towards the river to the beach, still some miles away. The view is stunning, with the land going gently away and the sea before you, silk and blue above a line of thick gorse, bursting into yellow. In this weather, in this heat, the gorse sometimes smells of coconut and honey, and you can hear the seed pods exploding in the sun with sharp snaps.

The scent comes to him and he hears far away the ducks in the water, and the Transit cutting back, he guesses, into the farmyard. Looking out over the sea he thinks of his son; he does not want to farm, but he'll know one day what a wonderful place this is.

A pheasant lifts in front of him, a claxon call – the call they always make, just twice, before thunder. He's losing his hunger to shoot now. Before, he would trace the line of the gun at his shoulder and imagine the shot and the pheasant falling. It's incredible how beautiful a pheasant is.

He sees, some way in front of him, a strange thing, something dead and crushed. He finds it is a rabbit, crushed and broken under the weight of broken bits of concrete. He stares, looking at it, thinking of the dog, hollow for a while. It infuriates him that men are capable of such articulate cruelty.

—

the Rabbit

The two boys had come along and found the rabbit dying by the bank. The breeze was up a little and it was nice because it had been dry for so long, and still; and the rabbit was wet and matted like a cloth, like a dog when it gets wet. At first they thought it was dead. It had the shapelessness of meat.

The boy saw it lain in the short grass by the bank, by the dry droppings and the scuff marks of other rabbits and the thick hard blackthorn above, coming into fruit.

'Hey, look,' said the boy. He didn't want his brother to see it, but he knew now the other boy would see it anyway so he said it.

The other boy stood away from the rabbit for a moment then edged to it and peered over it and neither of them were sad because the rabbit was dead.

The eyes were open and they did not move. Around them the breeze was going warmly through the blackthorn and the ticking sound of a tractor working came to them across the fields. Then the rabbit's eye moved.

The smaller boy went to prod it with his toe because he needed to understand better. He screwed up his face when he stretched out his foot. The eye moved slowly, just half-closing but not quite: as if it were willing itself just to close.

'Don't prod it, it's still alive,' said the other boy. The tractor ticked and chugged far away. They were both of them sad then but they did not want the other to see it. They stood around and nearly walked off and they knew it wasn't a right thing.

'I'm going to finish it off,' said the older boy. It was simple and brave, what he said.

When he said it the rabbit kicked but could not get up so it just combed round in a half-circle and it was like the rabbit was helping the boy to do what he said. Like it was trying to tell him with his desperation that it was the right thing. And they knew they had to kill the rabbit then because it was dying.

They looked around and there were some old stones by a wall and the younger boy picked up the biggest stone he could in both hands and looked at the older boy bravely because he was hurt when he saw the rabbit kicking and was confused and would do it himself.

The younger boy loved the older boy and would do it because of the way the older boy had said so quietly and straight that it had to be done and he knew that the older boy felt very sad inside, perhaps sadder than him.

'It might not die properly,' said the older boy. 'I'll try and not hurt it and just do it quick.' It made the younger boy feel sick when he knew he didn't have to kill the rabbit.

The older boy picked up one or two stones and they didn't feel right and then he found one which sat in his hand and thought it would be okay. The stone was warm and flat in the older boy's hand.

He always told the younger boy to do the things he didn't want to but this time he didn't; so the younger boy knew it was a very big thing they were doing.

The rabbit was twisted and all the wrong shape since trying to move and the boy knelt down close by it. He didn't want to touch the rabbit with his hands.

'Don't touch it with your hands,' he said, 'because it might be poisoned and we can't wash our hands.' He wanted to touch the rabbit with his hands so he could calm it so it could die gently.

He'd heard about this disease; how his mother's brothers when they were younger would have to go out around the farmland and would come back with bags full of rabbits that they had shot. They had to burn them. And he knew that the disease still happened, but not so bad.

He put his foot on the rabbit's shoulder to hold it down where he thought he should hit it on the neck and the rabbit's deep and sad eye opened at him and was deep and very beautiful. And the boy didn't show anything but inside he asked the rabbit if it was alright to do this and the rabbit's eye just half-closed in defeat, very slowly.

He hit the rabbit with the edge of the stone. He hit it as hard as he thought but he couldn't bring himself to want to hurt the rabbit, which was necessary, so the rabbit jerked under his foot and its back legs stretched and kicked. He hit it again in the neck where he had hit it before and there was a lot of muscle there and now the mouth was open and the tiny teeth showed, and the eye looked at him black and flashing with fear. Then he knew he had to hurt the rabbit and in him was the horrible slow panic of knowing something like this. He put the edge of the stone hard into the neck and just pushed and turned and tried to crush. He wanted the rabbit to die very much now and there was a click and the eye flashed and he knew it was done. The tiny mouth was gritted with strain and the teeth looked very sharp and white.

The younger boy was holding the big rock in both his hands up by his cheek and when he saw from his brother's face that it was done he dropped it away and it landed on the dry ground with a deep thud.

They didn't feel good about the rabbit dying but it was better. They took some old concrete from around the dry wall and took it over to the rabbit. When they went back to the rabbit it looked quiet and peaceful. The younger boy felt sorry for his brother and looked at him to see if he was okay and he was. The older boy told him about how another thing might take the rabbit and then take the poison; so they covered it up with the pads of concrete.

The younger boy put the concrete over the rabbit's head and wanted to walk away very quickly because his hand, for a moment, had brushed the fur; the older boy put the cement down on the rest of the rabbit and it wouldn't balance so he turned it over and rested it down. When he rested it down, the back leg moved.

When they walked away he did not tell the younger boy that the back leg had moved and told himself a lot that things moved after they were dead for a while because the nerves jumped. He'd seen his father skin an eel and even without a head it had jumped and twitched. He wished that he knew he'd killed the rabbit. He did not tell the younger boy that the back leg had moved because he knew that this knowing – the rabbit not dead perhaps and dying still under the heavy concrete – was only his; and he thought: 'if I had touched it with my hands I would have known for sure.' He knew then that people must be very strong.

The breeze was up a little and it was nice because it had been dry for so long, and still; and the two boys left the track and walked quickly over the low, green field, and the younger boy rubbed his hand where it had touched the rabbit's fur.

*

Chapter Five

the Tractor Wheel

Kate was not from here and she didn't grow up to be on a farm. When, years later, they found that Gareth had chlamydia – had caught it from the sheep – and this was why she'd lost the babies, Gareth was relieved. It fell on him. It was not a failure of her body and he hoped that Kate would not blame herself then. But it remained impossible for her to accept that some things die. After losing the babies, she felt every death.

She was checking the cows in the barn and she knew then that one had lost its calf and she was very angry with Gareth for not telling her. He had cleared up the bloodied hay but she knew there was a cow who should have a calf that did not have a calf after counting twice, after seeing the cow empty. She heard Dylan go off in the car.

You could hear cows placidly flicking flies away with their tails. The old wheel of the tractor was in the barn and she could almost feel the hard treads in her back. The sun was coming down on the corrugated barn roof and it was very hot inside, like in a greenhouse, and outside the sparrows were crazy loud, picking and fighting at the hay seed and dust-bathing fatly. But she was just very angry.

—

Gareth thought of her now. He doubled back up a dry track that was wide enough to take a tractor and had deep track marks so it was awkward to walk with his painful ankle. The sun had really come up now.

'I must never forget how perfectly built she is,' he thought loudly to himself. 'She is changing now, but it does not matter.' He'd meant simply to search the top fields, to rule them out, hoping for the vet to come then, and then return on the quad bike to the house; but he was walking, and it was as if he needed to walk.

He feels himself open his shoulders and hold his head up against the irritations of the missing cow, and the violence of the rabbit; he feels his body brace itself and challenge these things. 'It does not matter, she will change,' he thinks. And he knows that he must help her feel this for her to be well again. His body still demands hers, the familiarity of the map of her. The places of her that give softly when he holds her; that have changed and grown and shifted through the years, as if lilting with the changes of his own flesh, to be in tune still; as if he was the hard land and she the water that would always know it, however it changed. The things of her still fascinate him. It is true, he knows, that his man's chemistry will always want the tight trap of younger women, or the exoticness of a different skin – something other than he had; but he knew they would not have the smaller skills to satisfy him; would be over-aware, like strangers, be too full of thought to properly trick his body to the places he had reached with his wife. It is easy for him now to indulge his visual need for women – his son's magazines, the television, the magazines he has shyly for himself – but he never believed that they would, any of them, feel as good to him as her. He cannot imagine his body against the body of another girl. They had grown to each other and she had only ever been with him so he thought it was like she was only his shape inside.

He thinks of her perfect feet – how for years after they'd met she'd still kick off her shoes at every opportunity, to be barefoot. When did she stop doing this, he thinks. He did not notice. It gives him a strange guilt.

He thinks of his daughter's bare feet, and of the painted wellies she refuses to take off. He wonders how she will be, his daughter with strange green eyes from somewhere in their background, one or the other of them. Will she love like her mother? With belligerent decision. It scares him slightly. He knows his fear for her will grow as she gets older in a way it did not with his son, and he hopes he will not hurt her because of his fear for her.

But fear is rarely in context. In his father's memories it tells how he lost his first wife. The loss had a lot to do with his leaving the bank. He wanted to be on the land and see things live, and grow. His second wife was much younger and he cared for her greatly.

His father, every day, apart from the few months when he broke his leg, would cross the cows across the small road that ran between two pastures. It was when he was an old man, about eighty. He was crossing the cows one day when a police car brought his second wife back. She had been driving through the village and had put the car into the corner of a parked delivery lorry. She did not brake until the lorry came through the windscreen and the bonnet had been opened like a tin. When they checked her eyes they found that she had lost peripheral vision and was living as if she was in a tunnel. They found the tumour on her pituitary gland months later and took her miles away to hospital to die, though they tried to operate. Incredibly, because she'd always seemed so delicate to everyone, she lived. A few months later his father contracted bowel cancer and died in hospital after only three days, which meant he must have been in pain for a very long time. Gareth knew that he had died because he couldn't bear the thought of out-living the second woman that he loved.

---

the Car

The car just slumbers, like an old building, being taken over day by day more, by the brambles and grass where it's parked, which seems like an impossible place for a car to be anyway, as if it was dropped from the sky there.

The car, which has been everything from a spaceship to a tank, to the head of a large animal, still gleams though. Light bouncing, the white sheen of its runners and trim, even off the dusty windows. Because of the way the light comes off it, it seems as if it is moving, sometimes.

For years there were stories as to how the car got there, that far into an empty field. Even with brand new tyres, pumped to bursting, it was a mystery how the car drove past the hedges, over the marshy land. Dylan never remembered the tyres any other way than they were when he played in the car – dry, torn shards of rubber, like the bark that peels off an old tree around the wheel hubs that were rusting, so they looked like they were crumbling to the exotic earth you imagine in a desert.

There was the story of the burglars that had kidnapped Gareth's mother and driven off wildly pursued, until they were gunned down by his irate father with an old army rifle (leading to the story he'd been an undercover sniper, not a doodlebug spotter in the war).

There was the story of the flood – how the whole family had to climb into the car one day as the heavens came down, to escape a Biblical flood which left the car, as the waters receded, there in the field, and that's why the ground was still marshy.

There was also the story of the balloon. Which is the one they liked best, because of the photo. Of how

Gareth's father, as he told them himself, had built an enormous balloon and tied it to the car to travel around the countryside, high above the landscape. Whenever this story was told, Gareth's father would make a big thing of trying to find 'the photograph', looking here and there in drawers, until he unearthed an old postcard of a Zeppelin and, pointing to the carriage slung underneath, which was tiny in the photograph, would say: 'there's the car, you see'.

It never mattered to the children that the stories changed. They were equally true; they had their own theories anyway. The car was a playground.

Dylan hasn't been to the car for a long while, but years from now he will remember it as he drives past a convoy of Morris Travellers on their way to a vintage rally somewhere. And like all memories, that sit below us, out of the glare of our awareness, in shadow, the memory of the car will rush up, devastatingly. The red leather interior, in places busted, spilling stuffing; the windscreen wipers, which you turned by hand; the plastic padded sun visors; its perforated roof – like a teabag; the hot smell of the car and the broken floor, the sticky feel of the seats in the sun; the windows, that slid open.

It does not matter whether he remembers it accurately or not, this is his memory of it; and this is how it will live.

—

Gareth passes the car where his son used to play so much. He has to go back and tell his wife he loves her. For a second he sees the car as if it was new – the times they went for picnics in it – rising from the brambles, and only seconds later does his sense fill in the mouse droppings, and spiders, and the thick dust that is on the windows now.

He wants to walk back to Kate, and find her, and tell her very simply he wants her. He wants to love her with the clean love his father had for his wife. He knows she will be angry about the calf, which she will know about by now; and that she does not like her body, the way it has grown at the moment. But they have been through this before. After Dylan, when her body had changed and the pride of carrying was gone. She hated her body then, but to him she had grown more wonderful. Her ability to produce bewildered him, even though all his life he had been used to the processes of breeding. The things she hated most he loved. To him, her stretch marks looked like velvet brushed the wrong way, or wind across the grass. He wants her to be happy and to know that he does not want her to be any other thing but what she is; and she should walk barefoot again.

They should forget about the cow, and the children for a moment, and take off their shoes and go into the warm grass of the garden. He hopes very much that she is not going to be again like she was after the miscarriages, when she cut her hair all short and cut herself and would not speak to him for months. That was very hard. Thinking of it now it scares him that he won't have the strength this time to live through it with her. He worries about his ability to fight for things, when he is tired like this – from not sleeping, and from being worried always about tiny things – his ability to navigate a tragedy, or news of an illness. The world, he thinks, is filled with such unbelievable small heroisms which to him have always seemed far more remarkable than the huge heroisms of history. Somehow, we find the strength, he thinks.

He pushes this thought out of his mind, this suddenly subversive want for a tragedy to bring them back together, and he thinks of her walking in the fresh grass. He knows she will refuse at first and make ridiculous excuses of responsibilities: 'I have to do the washing', 'what about the cow?', 'you did not tell me of the calf' but he will persuade her, in this lovely sunshine, will pick her up and carry her if he has to so she laughs and he will put her down in the warm green grass without her shoes.

—

the Other Calf

He crosses the yard. In the hay barn sparrows are collecting hayseed and bathing in the dust – like they do in the cow barn, so the dust lifts and catches the sunlight coming through the wooden slats, dancing up in gold spirals. The flies buzz and tick. With the day properly here now, the swallows are high in the sky. As he comes into the yard, the heat seeming to rise off it already, the lost flight of pigeons explode into the air and are gone, hard over the house.

Kate is in the first field. He sees her pacing quickly at the gate, her head down and he can tell she is speaking to herself, to the ground, her hair tied off her face; and she is walking too quickly. He sees the problem as she looks up and meets his eyes, the blood on her arm.

'Where have you been?' It bursts out. 'The bloody cow has thrown its calf. I can't get it. I can't get it out.' She keeps on talking, cursing at him and the cow but he is already going to the cow.

—

The heavy brown cow was lying awkwardly back up against the bank. He ran to the shed to get the ropes and wished he had the bike to make things faster and to not hurt his ankle more and he knew she would be angry at him for not bringing the bike.

'Where the hell have you been. I thought you were coming straight back,' she was saying. He had the ropes now and was running over to the cow, wincing at the pain in his ankle. She stopped at the gate and did not come with him to help and he did not know why and he kept thinking about the blood running down her arm and the time she cut herself in the shower. She was still shouting.

The cow was a mess. The wet rod of the calf was half out, with one of its front legs twisted awkwardly still inside the cow. The calf seemed dead, but they often did and then they were alive when you got them out. He put his hand into the cow and tried to find the leg but it was all wrong and he knew the hoof had already cut the cow inside.

He had his eyes open but he was staring nowhere, trying to

visualise from what he could feel, the shape of the calf inside the cow. Kate was still screaming at him from the gate and he was trying to think. 'Where the bloody hell were you, you said you'd check the damn cows an hour ago so that's why I didn't check them. You should have bloody told me you weren't going to check the cows.' He looked briefly at her and she scared him; she was coming apart. He felt his patience snap in his stomach, the adrenaline of it go through him. 'Just go,' he shouted. 'Christ. Just go.'

The cow tried to lift herself as it sensed the things around her and he put his hand gently on the cow.

'Easy, easy, easy,' he was saying to her, his other arm on her haunch. 'Easy, girl.'

He brought the leg round and laid it along the calf's body inside its mother but he couldn't get it round enough to bring it out. He looked up again and Kate was gone from the gate but Emmy stood there scared and bravely watching.

He took the pulling ropes and closed the noose around the one free leg then tried to fix the rest of the rope behind the other shoulder blade. The calf was limp and its tongue now was flopping from its mouth. He sat back and braced his feet and pulled on the ropes, trying to gauge his weight in time with the contractions of the cow. He missed the extra traction of his little finger. Sometimes, it's the smallest things you lack. He could feel things give very slightly, a half inch won but brought back inside by the cow's big body. Then it came all at once, and the long black calf came out with the speed and sound of liquid. It was dead. He smacked it a few times but he knew that it was dead. Blood leaked thickly from the cow's gaping uterus. She panted slowly with the shock of birth. From the mark they'd made on her back, he knew she carried twins. The other calf inside her might be already dead. Emmy was by him now, looking at the dead black calf. It looked to her like a patch of wet tarmac on a new road.

'Mummy says she wasn't strong enough to pull the calf out by herself and that's why it died,' she said. He looked at her. 'No, love. This one wasn't made properly – look, can you see? It hadn't grown properly. It was dead already love, it just had to come out.' It played on him that this was the second death like this today and he knew now that throwing the other calf down the well was a problem. A fault in the stock? He thought of his wife. She was still shouting, he could hear her. Inside he wondered if it was his fault – if he had been too long. She came from a rural town and she was used to farms but she was not born to be on a farm as he was. He felt his anger go, this time; it had died down and receded.

'Go and tell Mum I need some soap and water and she might have to help me pull now. This one is a twin.' Emmy ran off up the field. She ran very importantly.

He ate alone. Kate had not helped him with the cow. He was sad that he had hurt her by shouting at her; but not sad because the thing was bad, more sad in the way we are sad when we hurt a weaker animal. He was sad about having more strength than her.

Dylan was supposed to have taken the bread crates back but he hadn't, so Gareth took the bread crates out of the van and hosed them down and enjoyed the cool water and left them against the wall to dry in the sun.

He came inside and soaped down his arm and the warm soft water felt good on him. He'd meant to get a gas bottle changed that week and there was a note on the cooker saying 'no gas' so he had bread and cheese. He'd tried to phone his son to ask him to collect more gas, but his mobile was switched off. So he left a message but knew he wouldn't collect the gas. He should ask the vet about the two dead calves, because there might be a big problem.

His wife was upstairs with a headache. He didn't know anymore whether he believed in these headaches or not. It was like she could switch them on and off, but he hated thinking this. He also thought that the violence of her anger nowadays could bring on these headaches. He thought: she is angry first, and it comes up as a headache, because there is nowhere for so much anger to go.

He tried to sip his coffee but it was filthy. Without the gas he couldn't warm the pan so he'd tried to heat it up by adding hot water from the kettle but it made it thin and weak and it tasted wrong.

He threw the coffee in the sink. It's not the headache making her angry, it's her. Her emotions are triggers, they trigger chemicals and she gets ill. It could just be her eyes, he thinks. He knows bad eyes can lead to headaches. But she won't have them checked. It could just be this constant heat. Her fair skin in the sun. He wondered whether he should go and see her but he knows it is better not to. She was like a grenade when she was like this. Simply going to her could be like putting back the pin, would diffuse her anger. Or she might just explode. In the rare times she was angry, Emmy was like this too; but she was so scowling and tiny and compact that she even looked like a grenade and they joked about it. When she was angry she was very furious which made them love her very much.

She sits at the table, drawing in her sketchbook now. Zebra watches her, and she talks while she draws. When she draws it is not with the excessive gestures of a child her age but it is small; as if everything on the paper is vital. The drawing overflows with details, so much so that she always must explain things to people when she shows them; the different instruments and inhabitants of the worlds she creates, which are always progressing somewhere, always in story, never strange, isolated still lives. If you asked her about her picture she always answered in colour: 'that's a red mushroom, a bright green dress'; but she never coloured in. 'I know what colours that they are,' she would say. She draws only from memory, she won't look and draw, as if the realness of a thing will destroy its place in her picture for it. She says she doesn't have the right pencils for the colours she sees.

Once, Gareth asked her about the tiniest cloud of almost unseeable dots. 'They're a cloud of lacewings that we saw today' she said, 'only they're so small you cannot see they're lacewings.' She always made distinctions between lacewings and fairies. There was no fooling her. When they had seen them that day, Gareth had said 'look, fairies.' 'No, they're insects,' she said, 'but I can see why a grown up thinks they are fairies.' To her, lacewings were just as magical as fairies anyway.

The first time they knew about her strangeness was when she came into their room one night and said, without being frightened, 'Mummy there's a man on the stairs.' 'You were dreaming,' they said, and asked her into their bed. After a while, she said perfectly sensibly 'there was a man, but he wasn't nasty. I was playing with my dolls and he talked to me through the door. I think he knows the little boy I see.' Since then they have learned to let her speak with these people. There is always a strange calmness to her, a sureness, as if she is listening always to an invisible music.

Now she's drawing a world of frogs and fairies: fairies underwater (which they can be, she says), and frogs and tadpoles and *half-frogs* – her word for them. He remembered her making the word.

the Frog Prince

They'd taken frog spawn from the pond in April before the ducks got at them. When the house came alive with tortoiseshell butterflies waking up. Two weeks later, more or less, the tadpoles hatched in the old glass tank; but it was three months or so before they grew their legs. Emmy watched them every day, from the moment they collected the frogspawn in a jar. They were constantly incredible to her. The black dots turning to the shape of fish inside the funny jelly, then the tadpoles hatching; and when the legs grew she pretended to believe that they were little people trapped inside fish. Gareth hadn't told her what they were.

The big ones ate some of the small ones, which horrified her, and she watched them change. It seemed a long time, to her, before they started to look like frogs and she guessed that's what they were, though they still had little tails.

They let them go in June. There was one though which had hardly changed yet from a tadpole, and which had not been eaten by the others. They thought it was simply a bad tadpole. But in June, perhaps July, it too began to change, but differently from the frogs, and when it took on the shape of a lizard Emmy was amazed. She thought it was a frog trying to become a prince.

Gareth remembers too the time he tried to explain to her about dandelions, which she loved – perhaps because of the magic of their changing too. Her love for things which weren't what you thought they were. She loved to play with dandelion clocks ever since his mother had shown her how to tell the time with them, this spurious decision as to time complying with Emmy's way of seeing the world.

She had spent a long time picking dandelion flowers one day and they were proudly laid out on her bedroom floor. When they hadn't changed to clocks by the next morning she thought perhaps it was because she kept peeking and magic only happed when you didn't look. Gareth tried to explain that they had to be alive to turn to clocks. 'But they are dead when they are clocks,' she said. 'Well, they've changed' he tried to say. 'They have to be alive to change.

The flower has to die to change into seed. They die to make more dandelions.' One dandelion dying makes a thousand new flowers. 'People don't do that, do they?' she said. 'No,' said Gareth. 'People don't do that.'

—

the Twin

Emmy had helped him with the cow – with bringing out the second calf which was a healthy brown calf. She had come back stumbling across the grass with a heavy mop bucket full of soapy water and a towel over her shoulder which kept slipping so she had to set down the bucket and pick it up. Then she'd heave up the bucket again with two hands and start again with the bucket knocking and spilling off her legs and over her wellies as she walked. She absolutely loved her wellies, even in this weather. She'd had the long important talk of children with her zebra and left him by the gate.

'Mummy's got a headache so I'm being her,' she said.

He'd heard himself think 'don't ever be her' and he knew underneath then that he would have to be careful now because the residue of his anger was still there and he didn't want it to come out. If it came out it would be very bad.

He made the rubbing sound with his finger and tried to read the paper but just thought. He had thought that the other twin would be dead too but it wasn't. While he was feeling inside the cow he was almost begging for it to be alive, to bring something good from this, and if it was good he wanted Kate to be there to see it turn good. Emmy was bending over the mother cow, patting the rolled knots of hair above her eyes and copying her father, saying, 'easy girl, okay girl.' From far away they heard another farmer calling to his sheep – every farmer calls a different way and if you are not a farmer you cannot call to animals without thinking you are stupid.

The calf came out and it was big and strong and healthy and it lay out panting and full with breath as he brought it round to its mother's snout so she could know it and clean her calf. Emmy still patted the cow's soft head saying 'good girl, good girl' and looking strangely at the new calf. He thinks of her doing this now as he sits at the table with the paper in his hands, and he thinks of her running to get the warm water.

*

Chapter Six

It feels like everything in my head is going to explode. If I move at all. Like if anything touches me I'll smash up. There's a sharp point of light coming in through a hole – a loose thread – in the curtain. It's like that sharp point of light, this pain; all of me crowds in on it, as if my whole life is just what is around it, a dark curtain. I shouldn't have shouted at Emmy.

I wish he would come up. I can hear him downstairs, laughing with Emmy. I wish he would come. I shouldn't get so angry, but he should have been there, he dreams too much. I know he is angry with me, but I wish he would come.

—

the Land Above the Road

She cares. She worries. She worries about him getting the land, and about her son in his car, and Emmy playing outside. She worries about Bill going mad and the gas bottle being too close to the cooker, and the calves that will die anyway and the sheep that fall sick.

She worries that one day they'll be too old to farm and he knows she thinks sometimes of a bungalow, but it would break him, her husband, and she knows that too.

He wants the land because he knows this, and he knows his children will not take on the farm; but he cannot bear to leave the place. If they have the land and put houses there, then they can rent out some of the fields and stay in the farmhouse on the money they make and maybe just farm a few things. But Kate worries about this. And she worries about all the things she has no say over, and he knows it's just her way of trying to feel that it isn't just random, that she has some control. But some things you just don't have any control of.

—

the Sedge

The cow went for a walk. She got up in the night and just walked and she was tired and slow by the time the sun came up, but a long way from the farm, for a cow. She just didn't want to be in the barn.

When she came to something, she put her great weight against it, and just leant, and let her big body crush the thing down, or break or snap it. If it was a hedge, she went into the gap she could find and let her weight smash through the small sticks and thorns and the dead, dry trees; and if it was a gate she'd just lean and push, so the thing gave, because many of the gates were not hung properly, and hung off their loose posts with pink string. She didn't do a lot of damage, as she didn't have horns. They cut off the horns at birth. When things gave way under her she just felt droll and programmed and just bewildered like cows are, and she just kept on walking, getting tired and hot in the sun.

She was heavy with calf. This was not her first year, so she knew what was becoming of her and understood the calf, but she didn't like the heat, or something, so she walked out of the barn. Her udder, gorgeous with milk, was scratched by thorns and the flies that followed her were landing on her warm hide and around her eyes, so she had to shake her head to move them.

For a while she stopped to eat, as cows do, just curling the long grass of a hedge into her mouth with her tongue. Her tongue was as big and pink as a baby's leg. The grass here was more lush than the hay and the short grass of the fields. By then, the cow had no idea where she was.

The sun had kept coming up and got hotter and the heat even came out of the ground, which had been under the sun for so long. The cow got down on a bank and scratched herself in the dust and lay down for a while and, what seemed like miles away, was the sound of duck going into the pond. The cow was grey and covered with dust now and warm in the sun by the bank. The birds played around her.

Later, the cow got too hot so she got onto her feet again and she could feel the calf moving inside her. She lifted her tail and let out a long wet pat. Then she went on. By now she was hanging her head when she walked and just ambling.

She walked into the bog, which is where all the cows seem to go, when they go, following their nose downhill, one foot in front of the other and other, wide hipped and plodding. When they get into the bog, they actually have to think. It wasn't so bad now, because of the un-easing dry weather and the constant sun, but mostly there was still mud, dotted with green weed and the footprints of birds and it wasn't the solid ground of the fields.

Thin willow and hazel was everywhere, so soon the cow started to crash and snap through it, but it confused her and took her strength. Underfoot, where it had dried, the bog was a funny shape and difficult to walk on. Going through the bog was very loud and sounded like twigs in a fire.

She walked into the bog for some time. Here and there a big oak tree had broken through the wicker of branches, and lifted up like a man standing on somebody's shoulders. Most of the bog was bare, the actual mud of the bog, but there were carpets of bramble in places, and tough sedge.

The sedge had dried and paled in the sun and was warm and long and the cow curled round and round in the sedge until it was a nest, and there she lay down.

Gareth lifts the cloth absently from the old table and smoothes the smooth grain with his hand. Some people like brand new things and other people like the things they've had for a long time. It is nicely cool in the house. They brought the table to the farm from the old house when they moved here. It was a big thing, putting the important table in the house. He looks at the plate of crumbs and the unwrapped cheese, starting to look plastic. Before, the family ate in the kitchen on the smaller table and the big oak table was reserved for Sundays and special dinners and guests. Emmy's drawing makes scratchy noises. When they moved to the farm, the family ate at this big table. He was thinking that it was not good that two calves had died, and there might be disease in the cattle. The cows were an indulgence, really. They grow just stock cattle now, which they raise and sell on to be grown up for beef, so it's important to have good calves.

Gareth looks at his daughter drawing – such a ferocious little sleeper – how importantly she ran. He smiles gently. Nine days from now she will start to die.

—

the Mushroom

Some of the bluebells will still be out.

Emmy will go into the woods with Zebra to play and she will find a beautiful white mushroom, come up after the rain. It looks to her like the dove that came. She will sit Zebra down, with the fairies around her, and have lunch off the table of a fallen tree. This is a secret place of hers.

She will think that she should not eat the mushroom, but she loves mushrooms very much and it is white like the ones in the field. It will taste different though, sweet like it smells and bitter all at once, and she will stop eating the mushroom and feel bad for picking it, so she will hide it, because it was such a beautiful thing before she picked it, like spoiling a flower.

The mushroom will be as big as her hand across, and shaped like the floppy felt hat one of her dolls wears, but shiny – like waxed paper. Its stem will look sort of shaggy (she will think, like the skin by Daddy's nails, peeling off), and there will be a big bulb at its base, as if it's in a bag. The white gills and the pure white of the mushroom will be like an angel.

She will find the mushroom nine days from now. In the night, she will wake up and vomit violently, and will be very thirsty. Like she's burning. She will call her mother and father. They will sit on her bed and pull up the covers round her and arrange her dolls and talk to Zebra while they touch her gentle head but she will not stop vomiting. Then the diarrhoea will start and she will mess the bed. The diarrhoea will come with great pain and it will feel to her as if someone is pulling her stomach with a huge, uncareful hand.

She will move into her mum and dad's bed. She will start to sweat hard and in hours she will look pale and haggard. She will look dangerously ill and it will happen very quickly.

They will call a doctor who will come out and know it's some sort of poisoning but will tell them that she is over the worst. That children's bodies react violently to even the little things to keep them safe. That it looks alarming, but it will be okay. He will tell them to try and let her sleep.

The vomiting won't stop and by the morning her hands and feet will go ice cold. She will be scared and anxious, like you are in fever, but she won't tell anyone about the mushroom because it was so long ago.

In the hospital where they take her because she will not stop trying to be sick and her whole skin will look pellucid and unnatural they will try frantic tests. They will also put a pipe into her stomach through her mouth and pump out the contents of her stomach but by then the poison will be in the other places of her body. Gareth will be sick with worry for her, and will not go to the auction. Then, two days afterwards, she will seem okay.

They will take her home and she will seem okay and the doctor will say that he was right and that she was just reacting violently to something because she was so little. There's all sorts of things on farms, he will say. It will seem strange and odd to them that she was so ill. Then violently and unquietly she will die.

—

Amanita virosa is deadly. It's the amatoxins which kill you, like the Death Cap. The other poisons, called phallotoxins, do nothing serious. *Amanita virosa* is called Destroying Angel.

A-amaritin – which is one of the amatoxins – hits the nuclear RNA in the liver cells, causing protein synthesis to stop, so the cells start to die.

When the poison moves through the kidneys, they try to filter it, but it attacks the convoluted tubules and, instead of entering the urine, it goes back into the blood. So it attacks everything again and again, breaking it down repeatedly and mostly it is better to die then. The little boy she sees comes to talk with her while she is dying, but it is still very bad.

*

Chapter Seven

There is an electric sound of birds.

The cow slept for a while, or slumbered, chewing the cud of the Timothy grass it had taken from the hedge, at the edge of the field. When she woke she was spooked. Birds hopped and snipped around her. She felt watched. She was very warm from the sun and she slumbered for some time. Then she got up and moved on. She clattered on, breaking back through the thick dry growth.

From the mud, like a broken machine, a cage of bleached white bones stood up. Many a cow had died in the bog, stuck and having to be shot where they struggled. You couldn't tell if the cow thought of her own death when she saw the bones. She left another long green pat as she walked; and for no reason, in no particular way, went on over the fields.

—

Gareth walked down to the bog. The heat is crazy. Everything seems subdued. Walking out after lunch was like walking into a wall of heat, and he couldn't see very much for a while, until his eyes accepted the light. He said: 'if the vet comes, you have to get Mummy.'

He went the way he thought the cow had gone, across the fields. He didn't know if the cow was in the bog, but the last time a cow did this she was in the bog. She'd made a nest and bedded down and had her calf quietly there.

From the road, above the land, he hears a dog barking, his neighbour's vicious shouts. The anger that is in him turns on them – the anger that is really because of the cow, and the rabbit, and his hurt ankle. He tries to put it on his neighbours. They are fat vicious people who don't know very much and don't like anything and it shows in their dogs. They came here some time ago, to Bill's farm, with the idea of using the land. But they did nothing, and let it ruin. He had tried to like his neighbours, but they were just not people you could like, in the end. He was sure one of their dogs had taken the cat.

They had lost the cat last summer and had said that she must have been taken by tourists. They thought this because there was always a chance the family that took her was a good family. A lot of tourists come here every year. Most of them are from cities and they don't understand the country – it is like a park to them. They see a cat and they think it is a stray because it isn't very close to a house.

So they coax it away, feeling sorry for it; worse than that, because they don't understand the way of things, the cat gets in the car. Like a kidnap. He imagines the cat suddenly in the city and being totally afraid, but he knows the neighbours' dogs had had it.

Once, one of the dogs – they are Alsatians and untrained and nasty – had come down the lane and was in the yard where Emmy was. It barked at her and ran at her and she stood stock still and it barked right into her face but she didn't cry or move. And Curly came out, old as he was even then, and tried to bark the other dog down but it just growled at him and inside Curly knew that the other dog could kill him. Then his son had come out and bravely ran at the dog which fled back up the lane, though it hesitated horrifically for a moment. They will be in the fields with the lambs one day, and Gareth will take a gun to them, and he will kill them. He will take the dead dogs back to his neighbours and if they say anything he will open all his anger on them because he is a very strong thing when he is angry.

When the neighbours got their dogs they argued about naming them. Their first ridiculous idea was to give them Welsh names which they could not say properly. They could not agree on names and in the end named one each, defiantly. So the dogs became tools they used against each other, like everything else about them. She named the bitch, with whom she shared some features, Cher, after the pop star; he gave his dog a lordship's name, which, in his voice which sounds like a chicken, he shouts across the fields because it's always *escaping*. The dogs fight constantly, too. Dogs are always a distillation of what their owners are. They learn by observing, not by being broken.

Sometimes, when he checks the stock at night, when he wants the night's long space, Gareth hears them fight, their angry voices tearing out over the fields and the dogs barking, like now, and it angers him, because it is a blasphemy to the easy quiet of this place.

—

the Monster

They used to say the bog was haunted, to keep the kids away. It was easy to believe, sometimes. Even now, in this dry world it had become, there was a presence to it, a sense of watching, a sense that it was waiting.

Gareth had found the pat, already drying, where the cow had rested by the bank. Bright orange flies crowded on it, preying on other flies on the dung, and laying larvae in it. He knew then she had headed to the bog.

He found the hoof marks in the soft mud that would usually be up to his waist, and impossible. The cow had crashed through, and for a while it was easy to follow the broken trail of her body. The ground looked starved. Gareth thought of the thing he had seen in a newspaper, long ago, of a three-year-old boy who had followed fallen-down trees and gone missing. He had followed the trees because he believed they'd been knocked over by a dinosaur, and he wanted to speak to the dinosaur. Gareth imagines him following the fallen-down trees, torn up on their sides from the ground. The boy was Scottish, he remembers that much. Sixteen hours later, they found him safe.

It's strange for Gareth to think of his father so far away, in Scotland during the war. He'd never really talked truly of the war and reading the memories it was odd to know he was posted to Wick and Dundee and Orkney, and Brighton and the Essex Marshes and Carlisle. He smiles at the thought of his father writing – 'when Hitler was doing all the evil and all the devilry a devil of his sort could do.' It sounded lovelier in Welsh – *a Hitler yn gwneud pob drwg a phob diawledigrwydd a allai cythraul o'r fath ei wneud.* He imagines his father saying it. He thinks how it must have been for him, posted to Wick, further than he'd ever thought to go, where he was made Chauffeur and Batman to the regimental Chaplain. Then, high in Scotland, the happiest three months of his war passed, driving round the locale with the Chaplain. He speaks of the time he was taken to see the Chaplain's ninety year old aunt, who spoke only Gaelic, which the Chaplain translated.

She wanted him to sing to her in Welsh. Gareth had only heard his father sing once or twice, and he imagined it must have moved her very much.

He stops for a while to rest his ankle, using it to loosely kick some old bones that lie like a cage, half buried in the firm mud. He desperately wants a coffee, now. 'Damn this cow,' he thinks to himself. He reaches down and pulls up a dandelion root and goes into his pocket for his knife so he can clean it, so the bitter juice will take his mind off wanting a coffee. It's such an automatic thing, reaching into his pocket, that he has to realise the Leatherman is not there all over again. He snaps the root, and uses his nail to scrape off the dirt.

Chewing the foul root he remembers the taste from his childhood – their rations – when his brothers and he played in the drainage ditches here by the bog. He'd passed the ditches earlier, dry and clear now and parched, like the inside of a shoe. The memory comes to him very strongly with the very strong taste, coming up clearly from inside him. It is like feeling, this. Memory and real care sit under the surface, like still reservoirs waiting to be drawn from.

It is easy, he knows, to take from the surface of these things, like dipping a bucket into water self-consciously: you can call up these things. But when it comes up un-beckoned, without self control, set off by some scent in the air, or fear, you can be shocked by its depth, which you hold in you all the time.

He knows that this is where his father got his quiet dignity, his ability to love so simply and so much. Through coming face to face with all this care in him. He thinks, if we have tragedy then we have to face care, like this taste makes me remember playing soldiers, and I can't help it. We have to admit our massive love for people. If we don't ever need to know its depth, we just feel the light on the surface.

When his father was young he married a girl he'd met and they were blissfully happy. Two sons were born. The bank moved him again and they had to leave the lovely house by the sea, but they were still very happy. A few months later another son was born. The birth was a good one, but a day before she was due home, his wife, Thelma, had an embolism. They tried to save her, but she died. His world was shot to bits. Gareth had no doubt that this was where his father's strength of care had come from, and his ability to be so happy at the very simple thing of a family.

He tries not to follow the tunnel of thought that is opening up before him like a big mouth. That perhaps a crisis would cure them too – would push away the tiny problems that were damaging them like splinters. Not the cow, or dead calves, or a son leaving for college, or the land he wanted, or her body not being wanted anymore. A crisis, that would reiterate the importance of life and of reaping happily from it what you could. Sickly, he thinks his father was lucky to have this.

Scenarios of disaster come to him, wash over him and he can't stop them. They are like storm waves and like a man in the sea now he has to try and ride them. He says to himself to not believe in fate, or of being careful what you wish for. The words 'I don't mean this, these thoughts aren't real' are like caught breaths of air. But now he can't stop the thoughts from hitting him. Perhaps, if it was brucellosis and it was in the herd, they would have to annihilate the animals and that would be the end of it and they could start again. The exhaustion of doing the same thing everyday would change. Or if something happened to just one of them that glued them all together – something they could survive. A car crash they walked away from, re-aware of the value of life. A quick pain; a quick, ready pain that reaffirmed the balances of want. Thoughts come to him violently, that it should be her to whom it happens, because the others have strength. The strength is needed in the people who stand by. Or else he wonders if an attack on himself would bring cohesion – make them realise what they could lose: a cancer he survives.

But underneath he understands that if he thinks these things, it means there's no strength there. And only if a tragedy occurred would he know if there was any left at all. How can one wish for cancer? In the coming weeks, it will all haunt him. A voice in him says: this is the simple cowardice that breaks us all eventually; a breaking of the surface strength. When you run out of the things that make you want. When you think of everything, of every other way to change a thing other than taking it head on. He just wishes Kate was better. That she would laugh, or walk unnecessarily in the sun, or simply love him back – which in the end amounts to tolerating what he feels for her. The idea of thirty more years with her... we live too long, he thinks. We're expected to love too much and too long. He mustn't be like this, he thinks, he mustn't let this dark thing take him: this ever-hungry, very close big cloud of not caring anymore, and of not wanting. This is the enemy which must be fought until the end.

—

the Vet

The vet came down the lane in his old van. It always amazed Gareth how such a quiet man could bear the rattling of that van; but then he understood the old vet had a tremendous respect for age. It was as if his still using it, and driving it, kept the van alive. He would not trade it in, and he would mend it when he could. Only when something massive went wrong with it would he give the van away completely. It gave Gareth a great faith in the quiet old vet.

The vet knew what he was like and accepted it. He would have been a doctor, but he knew that eventually the constant questions of people, their need for reasons, would wear him down; he would have to articulate things and explain the things he did, where in reality most of what he did he did from instinct, and animals just accepted this. He blew two short blasts on his horn.

Gwalch, the younger dog, barked and hopped at the vet when he got out of his van. Curly lifted himself heavily onto his feet and his tail wagged passively. A big, loud bee went around. The vet's eyes settled on the old dog and he smiled at him sadly and fondly and said 'hey, boy' very quietly.

The bee went around, and when it went close to the ground it drew up tiny little curls of dust. It was buzzing gently. 'They think now that bumblebees tread air, like we tread water,' thought the vet. It went round and round the small place by the door and if you could draw a line out behind it, it would look like a snake, with the same purposeful pattern of moving. 'They look curious, but they are careful finders of things,' he thought.

He felt the smallest tickle of something on his skin and had a fleeting smell of soap. Emmy giggled and another roll of bubbles floated out from her wand and over to the old vet. Curly wagged his tail more when he saw Emmy, and started to walk to the vet.

When Emmy heard the van coming down the lane she knew it was him and she had just put her head round the door and seen that her mother was asleep. So she went quietly back out.

'Mummy is with her headache in bed,' Emmy said. 'Dad's lost a cow.'

'So you must be in charge,' he said. And she gave a delighted nod. She thinks the bee looks like a helicopter.

There was more to what she said than beautifully bad grammar. It belied her logic. Since she was very tiny she'd always thought the best thing to do with any pain or worry was to go to bed. Because the thing that hurt you had to go to sleep as well. Then all you had to do was wake up very quietly, so you didn't wake the bad thing up. Then you got out of bed and left it sleeping, so it didn't hurt you anymore. Her parents had no choice but to accept it often worked for her, so they didn't question it too much, but they wished they could believe it too. One thing that had always fascinated Gareth was the way his children came up with things completely by themselves.

'Have you come to mend Curly?' she asked.

This hurt the vet a bit and he stumbled for a moment around the different things he should say. Then looking at the girl he just knew he had to be brave with her.

'I don't think we can mend him now,' he said. 'I think he's very old.'

'We should give him a good clean,' she said.

The dog was by the vet and he stank very badly. The vet could see the wet and shallow bite of the rat on the dog's foot, pussing and oily. It reminded him of the underneath of a tongue. The stink of the dog was bad. Because he was too weak to hold himself properly he'd messed on himself, and it hung in thick cords from his long fur.

'We keep giving him a bath with the hose but he just gets dirty again,' explained Emmy. 'I think he needs a haircut.'

The dog looked benignly up at the vet, panting happily. Killing the dog would be more difficult for him to do because the dog had not accepted it was time now. He wished that Gareth was there. He respected these people. He respected that they had not asked him to come and kill the dog as soon as it begun to smell; as soon as the grotesque tumour had started to make them feel nauseous each time they saw the dog.

The vet looked down at the bee, which had settled on a dandelion. It had a bright, golden collar and yellow and white patches at the end of its body so it looked proud on the dandelion. If the vet looked more closely he would see it had more body than usual, seemed more armoured, had less of the thick soft fur. He knew they lived in colonies much smaller than honey bees, of around one-hundred and fifty. Drones and workers looked after the solitary queen in a nest under the ground in an old mouse hole, or something like it. They take moss and grass inside it, and build wax cells for the honey and eggs.

If the vet looked more closely at the bee he'd notice it was un-busy, not collecting the bright pollen from the flower into sacks on its legs. It was a cuckoo bee. They look like another bee but they aren't, and they go into the colony of the bee they look like and kill their queen. Emmy watches the bee a minute. When they lay their own eggs, the host workers look after the cuckoo bee, and because they all die in the winter it is futile. Only the cuckoo bees survive, hibernating through the winter and waking later than the bumblebee queens to give them time to make their nests. But the vet doesn't notice so much, because he is thinking about the old dog.

'I'm going to give Curly an injection that will make him sleep,' he said.

'Will he wake up?' asked Emmy, already understanding.

'No. He won't wake up,' said the vet. 'Do you want to help?' Curly huffed and snapped his mouth at the bee. When he was younger he used to love to chase bees.

They took the dog to the place where he normally slept in a part of the old milking parlour and lay him down. Curly had followed them and they walked slowly for him. It was excruciating, how full of hope he was. The dog had the look of a thing which loved things utterly and would be forever pleased. He settled down in the hay to sleep.

'What's in the injection?' asked Emmy. He didn't want to say. Brutally, he had a picture of the little girl leading the dog round by the ear, many years ago.

'It's a medicine that will make his heart go slower and slower; and then it will stop.' He didn't have to say that it wouldn't hurt the dog because of the way he said this thing.

'Like when it stops raining?' she said. Nothing had ever moved him more in his life than the beautiful questions of children.

'Yes. Like when it stops raining.'

Far away Gareth had heard the horn and knew the vet had come and he'd started straight away to walk back to the farm. Trying to move quickly through the bog, even though it was dry, was very hard. When he heard the vet's old van grumble into life and the stretch of tyres over the loose grit in the yard he knew the dog had been put down. He looked up the slope towards the farmhouse and could see the dust rise off the lane where the old van threw it up. Then he turned back again, and went back towards the bog.

---

the Cow

The cow walked lazily up the track between two rails of blackthorn. She'd heard the vet come and go. She hadn't liked the bog, which for a long time had been full of *hide-*

behinds, which were brought across from the lumber camps of Wisconsin, and which Gareth's father had learnt about from the American troops he served with. No matter how quickly you turned around, how hard you looked for them, these creatures always stayed behind you, so no one had ever described them. The cow had only sensed them. She was slightly demented now. She felt she should give the calf but her body wouldn't. It was a strange feeling to the cow. Her breath was rasping, and she was puffing loudly through her nose.

She kept walking in the sun and grubbed the hedge here and there because now the flies were driving her silly, landing on her face all the time, and the cow was very thirsty. She was trying to find water now, and just walking.

*

Chapter Eight

the Beast

They said there was a beast in the bog. There was a whole fauna created to keep the children away from the dangerous places, but they were told of with amusement, incredulously, so that the thing was a game, and the children could play the game of staying away from these places without being drawn to them, by being curious of fear. Gareth did not know that he could tell these stories until he told them, and it delighted him. But he had grown up here, and had been allowed always to make-believe, because the countryside does not refute pretend things in the brutal way a town does.

The beast in the bog was like a kangaroo, but with the feet of an elephant. It didn't have the head of a kangaroo though, the long, rabbit-like face. Its face was like a pug's, smashed into a grimace, with its tiny eyes not telling you how it felt. Only its teeth could give away its emotion. Needless to say, the beast fed on children.

A snake lived in the slurry pit, except it wasn't so much a snake, more a being of muck and skin that moved and bloated like a worm dropped in a puddle. It demanded feeding, all the time, and lived on a diet of poo from the cows. It's why they kept the cows, they said, to make poo for the snake, so he didn't consume the farm. So it was that Emmy came up with the theory that she knew which cows produced more poo than milk, from the black and white ratio of their bodies. You should never go near the pit, they said.

Gareth had fought with the beast from the bog and the beast had taken his finger. When they did go near the bog, Gareth showed his children the bones and the leftovers of animals so they knew the truth of the stories. It is hot now. It drips with heat. This damn cow, he thinks. A dry heat like holding your hand close to an iron.

—

He thought hard about the dog. He was sure he had not hoisted death on him, that it really was time. That they hadn't had Curly put down because, though they tried not to admit it, he had begun to repulse them. Animals are put down for the sake of their owners. He did not believe that animals complicated pain in the way humans do. He'd also watched animals for long enough to know that they fight death violently, or else simply lie down and die. He believed in dignity though, that this was a right in life not just human. He knew that having Curly put down was about dignity. He hoped that Emmy would not be too sad and was sure Kate would have explained things to her gently, while the vet was there.

—

But Kate slept. Sleep turned the pain for her. Awake, it was like a kettle of rolling water; sleep turned her pain to steam.

She thought of Gareth's finger, shining like a healed blister. She thought of his shoulders and the cords of his arms, and the rough hair. Compared to her body, she loved his body, like she loved the exquisite smallness of her daughter, and the broadening shoulders of her son. She loved them physically, as objects; but she could not love her own.

As she lay asleep she thought of her son stretching into his long life and of her daughter growing and becoming more beautiful and complicated, like one of her pictures, as life added to her. She thought of the farm, turning. She felt the headache starting to clear.

—

Dylan

Dylan had come back and couldn't find Emmy and found his mother sleeping in bed. It was a while after the vet had been but he didn't know about the dog. He could not believe his father was still looking for the cow.

When he got back to the farm he turned on his mobile after driving and found that he should have got a gas bottle and figured there would be nothing nice for tea. His mother in bed and there being no gas it would just be cheese and leftovers and bread. He should go and get the gas but he thought – it's too late to go and get gas now, on a Saturday. Because it was summer there were a lot of camp sites open and he would have got gas very easily, a small bottle at least. But he didn't think of it because he didn't want to go out and get gas.

On the lane he'd seen a family of stoats, playing in the dust. They were no longer than his hand, bounding loose and cantilevered along the track, now and then ambushing each other, lifting and watching, bouncing at the passing flies or overhanging heads of grass. Watching them, it was difficult to recognise they were capable of killing things twice their size.

He knew he should go and help find the cow, or find Emmy and play with her, but inside he felt not part of the day that had happened here. He had gone to see his friends all day and when he drove back into the farmyard the whole flight of pigeons had taken off from the yard at the sound of his car. He walked into the house and he could just tell it had been *a day*.

He picked up his car keys because he felt very far away all of a sudden, and he went again. In a few years he will want to be back on the farm, but for now he left a note saying 'gone out, hope that's ok' on the table.

—

the Pigeons

As he drove away the pigeons went up into the air again. The curious slowness of pigeons on land; their energy in the air: like two different animals with two different purposes. The white dove looked like a flower amongst them. The family wondered if the pigeons would ever go, would leave one day as strangely and as together as they'd arrived. They seemed to bounce and tilt in the light.

In a pigeon's cells, somewhere in their head, tiny magnetic crystals survive, tiny pieces of iron ore called *magnetite*. Invisible lodestones, tinier than dust, creating a compass, sensing polarity, the inclination of magnetic fields around the earth.

The electronic particles in the crystal, moving between different ions in a structured path, turn the ore magnetic and tell the pigeons their way. They've also found this in the brains of bees.

They've found iron too in their otolith organs, in their inner ear – the things which give them a sense of where they are in the air, of the space they move through. If the earth's geomagnetics are wrong, they get lost.

It makes you wonder what crystals run through us, what drops of salt? Because something in us gives us a sense of where we should be, too, if we listen.

the Nest

On the walk back to the bog Gareth had tried to think of something else and not the dog, so he thought about the land he wanted, and how he himself would try to build, or just sell the plots. The finance was arranged well past the guide price, but he knew he shouldn't be eager and carried away if the land got too much. He tried deliberately to think about the land, but he kept thinking of the heat, and Kate, and of the dog; thoughts that were like sounds. Of Kate's white body. Time alters things, and it is right and good that things change and he accepts her body changing in the way he accepts the changing landscape around him. He is aware now that his care for her outweighs his want, and he knows she feels this as a lack of hunger. Maybe it is different for them, he thinks, different from a man. If you are hungry for a woman it is because you are hungry for women, but you can care for just one.

To buy land at auction you get the catalogue and a lot number and you carry out your searches and surveys. Gareth hadn't had the land surveyed and had argued with Kate about this, saying 'I know the land, it's the same as ours, just a road between them.' You must have all your finance, surveys and searches complete prior to the auction because at the fall of the gavel you enter into a binding contract to purchase that land. You should seek planning consent in principle first but Gareth has not, because he knows there will be no planning given yet, and he knows how easily ideas get around in this place, and he is hoping no one else will think of this purpose for the land.

While he waits for the time to come for planning, he will use the land to graze, with the extra room perhaps even increase the sheep, and it will pay for itself that way too. 'It is a crazy idea,' says Kate, and thinking of her saying this makes him scratchy again. Perhaps it is just a crazy idea, just a crazy idea, he thinks.

He should clear this scrub and use this land. He gets determined to do this whenever he's down here. All the unfulfilled plans he had, like the plans we have with a lover that never come to anything. Take away the thin growth and the struggling plants and let the land dry out. It would be like writing memoirs, he thinks. Choosing what stays, and giving things space to grow again. The willow just comes up so quickly and the roots, which you would think would drink the water, don't; they dam it in the ground, turning the ground to bog.

If you take down the trees, the land dries out, and the water starts to drain away. Now would be a good time to do this, with the bog so dry already. He could have four more fields a few years from now. The bog. The stink and dark and the effort of it. And we wouldn't lose more cows, he thinks. He's angry he missed the vet. This damn bog makes you lose any sense of where you are. I want Kate to want me, he is thinking, and suddenly, like light breaking the clearing, he knows what it is he must do. He knows it clearly and well. He should just walk. Just walk and keep walking, away from it all, and not stop.

He swallows his anger and says again to himself 'this will be just a phase, it's just a change, and I didn't mean to wish those things I thought earlier' and while he's thinking

'I didn't mean what I just thought' he finds the big comfortable place the cow has made. When the cow is not in there he knows inside he cannot look for her anymore. All I have to do is keep walking. 'I could go. I could just go,' he thinks.

*

Chapter Nine

the Tractor

The tractor had been on the farm almost since Gareth's family got there. When they bought the tractor, it was brand new.

Henry Ford had made an unsuccessful attempt to design tractors back in 1907, then went at it again after war broke out, in 1915 – a more concerted effort, backed by Ford mass-production principles. There was a great need for machines on the land, given the men and horses who had gone to war.

In 1917, production of the Fordson F started, solely to answer the needs of the Great British government. In just over ten years, nearly three-quarters of a million were sold, more than ever before or since of one tractor. The Fordson F was the most influential design in tractor history and only the most solid manufactures survived in rivalry against it.

At the Smithfield Show in 1951, (the year Gareth's father left the bank), Fordson unveiled their new Major E1A. With an easy-starting diesel engine, economical and reliable, it demolished demand for petrol-vaporising oil tractors, but there was clearly demand for a smaller machine. So in 1957 Fordson launched the Dexta.

Bill has it now. They needed a bigger tractor on the farm since and had a new Massey years before. One of the first things it did was take Gareth's finger, as if it wasn't tame yet. For a long time, the Fordson sat under the 'ramp' – the building Gareth's brother had built to practise his car mechanics and fix the farm's engines (that brother had a garage in the north now). In the winter, long icicles that they used to drink and play with hung from the roof of the ramp, but right now this heat made it easier to imagine a unicorn than an icicle.

The tractor's bright blue paint faded and flaked and the iron of it rusted; the exhaust corroded so much you could put a finger through it, like it was pastry; but still the tractor had a personality. The children would play on the ripped seat, bouncing up and down as they pretended to drive. Emmy liked to give it a bath. And once in a while, when the mind took him, Gareth would look over the engine and would admit that it was still a good engine, and a strong thing, and it should be working, like a person who is strong.

So he gave it to Bill, who helped him clean up the tractor again. The Dexta was the last to bear the Fordson name. It would be a shame if it had become another iron skeleton on the land.

—

Bill tocked up and down in the tractor, trying to break up the ground with a chain harrow. He had seen the vet come and go and had hoped nothing was wrong and had waved at the vet because he knew him. Though it was very hot, Bill wore the same things as he always wore, and the sweat came off him thickly.

The cow by now was demented with flies and the weight of the calf in her and the hot relentlessness of the sun and she let out a big, thirsty bellow. Over the hills the day's haze built up. She was tired of only being able to move in a certain way because of the weight of the calf and wanted to buck and kick as if that would get rid of the heat of the sun. It was nearly evening now but was still hot. The redness of her coat looked golden in the sun.

She was walking on, trying to find a trough of water, thinking I'll walk on for a while but I could just lay down and sleep and she didn't know where she was. She had the droll, shaking head of an idiot. She was thinking about crashing herself into the bank and the fence to be insensible and get out of the heat, and of doing crazy things cow's shouldn't and she pushed blindly at a corrugated iron sheet in the hedge that just bent underneath her. She could hear the tractor. She let out another long moo and crashed down the hedge. The iron sheet had been all day in the sun and was hot on her udder, and that's when she found Bill.

I think where he is. I think what I'd do if he left me. If he didn't come back. If he decided to just go away.

I should have looked for the cow. Should have been with him. It might have been nice, in the sun. I look at him and I know I have been lucky because he is a good man and I love him very much but it makes me feel sick what I did. And sometimes when I feel his hands all I can think of is the other thing and how when it was happening it felt good, and it makes me feel sick thinking that. And though I know that chlamydia can come into a man without his knowing it, sometimes I think of the illness he was putting in me every time we made love, and I hate him for the babies I lost. But without him. I cannot think of being without him.

—

the Dandelion

He kneels down by the dog and strokes his hand through the thick hair. The way he lies looks unbearable. He looks at the vicious cut on the foot, which the vet has put a powder on to stop it weeping, and is horrified by the tumour which looks as if it still has life, will still grow on the dog. He can't bear to touch it. He thinks of it as a great thing which latched onto the dog to draw it down. It is horrible for him that this thing has come from inside the dog. 'There boy' he says softly, and he sees Emmy in the sunlight by the doorway.

He thinks of her as a younger child, dancing on the grass, turning around and around in the sun with the dandelion clock she holds casting its seeds around her.

He hears her giggle all those years ago – sees the huge, massive quietness of the way she smiles.

She comes over to him and touches him with a cat's instinct for paper.

'He was very good,' she says.

'They put Curly down,' he said to her. He'd just come into the room and stood for a very little while and then said very simply 'they put Curly down.' Then he stood a bit more and went out because he didn't know what to do.

She sits on the side of the bed and accepts that the headache seems to have gone. The scene of her illness is around her. The half-drunk cup of chamomile. Aspirins and water. An abandoned magazine open loosely on the floor by the bed, the dark curtains drawn. The unnecessary hot water bottle kicked out in the afternoon heat. Now the pain is not there, she wonders briefly, lucidly, whether it was real. It's hard to recall pain when we are not in it. We remember it vaguely, descriptively, by making it live almost, like a creature, giving it some deliberating quality.

They seem to have two ways of bringing her down, these headaches: the sharp point of today, which makes it as if she can only know the world through it, like looking out of a pin-hole; and a weight. A weight that is heavy like mud: that first brief and dull feel when you hit your head, but staying that way, not developing, just numb, heavy, until it seems to break off like a beach cliff and slide down one side of her body in a slow avalanche of pain. Then they just seem to go.

—

the End of the Memories

Gareth pours himself a glass of water and looks out of the window by the sink over the bird feeders and scattered hay and dust of the small space outside, before the lawn. Their water comes from the spring and comes cool even now.

In a few days Gareth will come to the end of the memories which end when his father got to the farm. He will wonder if his father knew for some time of the cancer in him, and so put things down, choosing what mattered the most. It will feel odd to him that the memories stop when they moved to the farm, because, really, it is where his own memory begins. The end will say: 'so in 1951 I left the bank and went into farming. It was seen as a deeply foolish thing to do by many of my peers and today I'd have to admit perhaps there was a good deal of truth in that. But now, in my old days, I have no regrets about the choice –

my wife and children would agree. And what else is there to life other than following the path which brings pleasure and interest to you, without counting the cost or loss, but delighting in those things which are desirable, and which bring you happiness.' And Gareth will wish very much for this happiness.

'These damn things. These damn niggles,' he thinks.

the Dunnock

That year, in that space, that patio, every day a hedge sparrow came to eat the scraps of bread and fallen shreds of nuts and lard that came down from the two bird feeders hanging in the laburnum close by in the hedge. From one side it looked perfect; but on the other you could see a bubbling growth, like a collection of salt, that was on its beak and eye. It was disquieting. Tiny, but still nearly monstrous. It came when the other birds had gone. The next year, it would not be there.

—

He turns round with the cool glass in his hand. Kate is there.

'Now you're up.' She is in her dressing gown, and is holding the wet flannel she had put to her head.

She says 'I'm sorry' and she says it in a way that doesn't mean she's sorry. It was like a question.

'Now you're up. Emmy had to deal with the dog.'

'Yes, you told me.' He'd thought she hadn't registered.

She waits. 'My headache.' She still feels frail, like a glass valve.

'Emmy had to deal with the dog,' he says again.

She stood there red-faced and pale. He thought she looked feeble and it made him hate her right then, because he couldn't believe it. How much I don't want you just now, he's thinking.

'You should have called the vet in the morning yesterday.'

He holds his anger in, but it's like the far off rattle of a loose wheel. 'I was in the bank in the morning.'

'Yes, your dream.' She is cruel, the way she says dream.

'– – I didn't find the cow.' They are quiet. He stays by the window and drinks the glass of water. He was so angry that she stayed in bed while the vet killed the dog.

She starts to clear up, talking under her breath, getting a wind of argument up under her.

'I'm not obsessed, Kate.' She'd mentioned the land.

'The dog should have died yesterday.' Already they were distancing the dog by not using its name. 'You should build on our land.' He just looks at her.

'It's our land.'

'Bill uses it.'

'He's simple, Gareth. He doesn't do anything.'

'My father gave him that land and I won't take it from him.'

'We could fit houses there.'

'We could fit houses on the land.'

'Land we can't afford,' so full of poison.

'The bank will lend.'

'And what if they won't give us planning?'

Christ, I should just go from this, just go, he thinks. To let all my anger out would be like cool water. She sees the change in him, and changes tack, uses weakness.

'I'm just worried,' she says weakly. 'I worry that it will go wrong for you. I care about you.'

the Fight

'You use care like a weapon,' he says. It's like a greenhouse breaking.

—

After the fight they were quiet. 'I have to take the bread crates back,' he said, and he drove off in the van.

*

Chapter Ten

Gareth comes in through the front door and puts the torch on the shelf in the porch.

'Bill brought the cow,' she says, and they try to talk.

—

Bill had seen the cow and stopped the tractor and gone to help the cow. He'd always had a quiet way with animals. He saw she was heavy with calf and helped her down through the hedge where she was stuck on the corrugated iron. She came on her haunch down from the hedge with her big bag, streaked and marred with blood, clopping with her, like a balloon full of water. She hissed and puffed through her nose and even then, being a cow, she reached round and pulled a long tongue-full of grass from the hedge. Bill checked over the cow while she crunched the long grass.

When she had drunk long and hard from the buckets Bill brought from the water butt she got to her feet and she dashed a short way as the madness of sense came back to her. She shook and bucked but Bill spoke to her gently and soon she lowered her head to the grass and rubbed her nose on the short turf and started to follow his voice. Bill was clucking and speaking and the slow cow came with him. Soon the day would come to an end in a broad and brave sunset, like it was angry at its finish. The evening was beautiful with the glittering sea and the sun specially lighting some of the far hills.

It was a long walk that day for the cow but she came back to the farm and she and Bill were in the yard when Kate found them and the swallows were flying lower now with the change of pressure in the air. Bill was stroking and patting the roan cow and dust came off her into the evening.

'Hot day,' says Bill. 'Hot day.'

---

the Earth

He cannot sleep much after the argument. She lies next to him, tense in the way she has now when she sleeps, the corner of the thin sheet held over her mouth in a tight knot and every now and then her arm jumping, or a sharp inhalation of quick breath. It's like she's scared now, when she's asleep. It's difficult to be by her.

The sleep he gets is snatched, is not caught safely enough to take him into proper sleep and it is more like opening his eyes momentarily on a violent film: there was a quick nightmare. Rats attacking the dead dog's face, taking his eyes and his tongue, and opening the big growth so the sick grey cells spill out.

He gets up and pulls on his shorts and the old jeans and throws the day's t-shirt back on. His mind is too busy. He can't bear to think of Curly lying in the straw beside the old tractor wheels and fertiliser sacks and the broken machines. The thought of his old dog beats everything out of his mind and he can't think about the argument, or shouting at her, or the next day or the unhinged gates. He is horrified by the thought of the dead dog lying there; it feels unfinished like this. He does not want to wake up in the morning and need to bury the dog. The image of the rats taking him comes back to him.

—

The ground is very hard and there's still warmth in the night. It feels close and oppressive and unfresh. The ground is hard but the hard work soothes him as he brings the *caib* into the ground. The digging is hard without a finger, and his ankle still hurts when he puts pressure on the spade to move the soil; but all of these things help him work. Gradually, the earth breaks up, scattering dust and small stones in the thin light of the Tilley lamp. The Tilley lamp hisses as it burns and gives out a silver light. Around it, moths and lacewings start to come.

He'd taken the Tilley from the porch and filled it with sharp pink meths. It's a smell he's loved since being a child, when the smell of the Tilley was with them in the lambing shed, or a few times late out in the garden. Some of the meths was on his hands and evaporated quickly, leaving his skin strange and dry but supple like a belt.

He pumped pressure into the lamp and lit the mantle and the thin silver light spread out.

He lifts the dog down into the hole he's made. He looks like a big proud dog in the hole. Covering him up is very difficult but it is right. There's the slightest change in the air.

On the flat hard ground by the place he has dug, the raindrop lands and disappears, seems to be drunk up by the dry earth. He holds out his hand and the rain starts to fall. The drops flash in the light of the lamp and spread on the ground.

And then it really rained. The rain came down on the corrugated tin of the porch roof and fell into the dry, cracked soil and onto the wide fields.

Kate rose from bed and went over to the window. She leaned out and she let the rain fall on the bare skin of her arms. It seemed as strange as snow.

On the stairs she hears him, and she knows that he is

coming lovingly to her; that there is no malice now. She leans her head out of the window and when she turns back into the room the rain is on her face and her hair, and runs down her neck into the soft cloth of the shirt. She starts to cry. He is strong and proud and good.

'It's raining,' he says, and she can hardly hear him.

Acknowledgements

The 'memories' that run through the book are taken from *Hen Arferion a Hen Gymeriadau*, recorded to tape by my grandfather David Llewelyn Williams before his death in 1991. They are given either faithfully, or I have used them and turned them to the purpose of the story.

The section 'The Rabbit' is for Sean Kelly, who was there.